ISBN 978-0-9813148-4-1

KDP ISBN 9798374664140

Credits:
Edited by Sukriti Sachar
Technical Support by Maanvir Singh Mann
Cover Image: Image: Freepik.com.
This cover has been designed using assets from Freepik.com

To the memory that was
our son
Bruno

CONTENTS

FOREWORD

It gives me great pleasure to introduce the short stories of Mukhtar S Sidhu.

A word or two first about Mukhtar. He was born in Village Raqba in Ludhiana District of Punjab in 1926. He graduated from and trained as a teacher in Punjab University. He taught in various schools in Punjab and Himachal Pradesh before migrating to Canada in 1969. He completed post graduate courses in Psychology from Dalhousie University, Halifax and taught in Halifax County from 1969 to 1985. He now lives a retired life at a monastic Dera and at Shimla, writing dry, wry, funny, ironic stories. Lucky man.

The tone of these tales is young despite the writer's maturity. Though their subject matter is varied, they all reveal the sharp, distanced vision of an outsider. It is the tone of someone who has been away for long, and then returned to be enriched by the presence of several worlds in his head.

Enjoy yourselves.

Upamanyu Chatterjee

New Delhi

Dated: 14 September, 2009

INTRODUCTION

It was the year 2005, four days before Diwali, I was being wheeled to the operation theatre of Fortis Hospital in Mohali, Chandigarh, India for a major intestinal surgery at age 80. Dr. Shashanka Bose was the surgeon. I was fully aware of the seriousness of the operation.

Thoughts crowded my brain, each one struggling for space. One stood out prominently, demanding immediate attention: If my body comes out of the operation theatre feet first, will I, the surviving soul, have any regrets as to how I lived my life? The answer was prompt: I could have given a lot more love to this world than I actually did.

Since then I have been fully alive to the stark reality of my commitment to the balance of my life: I am on a mission.

Most of the stories in the collection "When the Azaleas are gone" were written between 1969 and 1985 when I was a teacher in Halifax County – Bedford District, Nova Scotia, Canada. In some of the stories I have felt more comfortable using first person as the story teller. These varied characters have no semblance to me as a person. In one such case the first person, I, is an uneducated person, in another, the first person makes a living as a writer. The stories and the characters are pure fiction.

Mukhtar S Sidhu
June 4, 2016

ABOUT THE AUTHOR

The Bhatti rulers of Jaisalmer stood by Maharana Pratap againt the mighty army of Akbar, the great Mughal Emperor and were defeated. Hounded and persecuted by the Mughals, the Bhatties turned towards Punjab. The princely Sidhu states of Punjab were ruled by the descendants of the Bhatties.

One of these warriors, along with his wife and four sons came to a small pond of fresh water where the wooden axel of his chariot broke, making any further progress impossible. He spent the night by the side of the pond and early next morning he rode his steed to encircle as much territory as he could before sundown. He declared that the raqba (area) covered was his property. The village bears the name Raqba. It is in the Ludhiana District of Punjab.

I, Mukhtar S Sidhu, am that Rajput warrior's direct descendant. I am the son of the Late Sardarni Bahadur Fateh Kaur Sidhu, (1888 – 1992) and the Late Sardar Bahadur Captain Hazara Singh Sidhu, OBI, (Order of British India) (1888 – 1947).

At one time, I owned two sizeable apple orchards in Kulu, when it was a part of Punjab. Later, Kulu and I were adopted by Himachal Pradesh.

I migrated to Canada in 1969 and taught school from 1969 to retire in 1985. Now I divide my time between India and Canada. I spend my time writing English short stories, and English and Urdu poetry. I have also written a book on mysticism which will be published soon.

My two sons, two grandsons, four granddaughters and eight great grandchildren live in Canada.

Mukhtar S sidhu
310-2955 Diamond Crescent
Abbotsford, BC Canada
V2T 2L5

when the azaleas are gone

and

other stories

The Big Top

Take off the mask and
The multiple layers of makeup
Take a long, hard look.
I bring you your lost mirror.
Hey, don't look away 'cause
I am talking to you.

It was a big top. If anything, it was a big top: not any run-of-the-mill marquee. It was **the** big top.

If you are not a New Delhiite, Old Delhiite or for that matter, a Delhiite (*Dilliwala*) of any brand, I will bet you a night out with my fun-loving young secretary that you have never seen or heard of such a monstrosity before. I have not checked out the terms of reference with my secretary but knowing him well as I do, I am sure he will play along.

Considering that cities in India are discarding the names bestowed on them by the British during the period of the Raj and are reverting to their old identities, it is surprising that Delhi the capital city of this nation, with its ten million plus humans (at the time of writing and not at the time when you read. Remember, we have the reputation of breeding like flies.) is still yearning to be called Dilli, the city with a heart.

The monstrosity referred to was a mega-tent with a multi-storey look. These relics of the dead Arabian-Nightly past have suddenly re-emerged on the Delhi scene. You couldn't walk on any of the floors except, of course, the ground floor. All the same, the sham of several floors was there. The upper 'floors' were designed, in an intricate fashion, like multicoloured balconies, adorned with satin and lace and overlooking the spacious ground floor enclosure, giving the tent an exaggerated fairytale look. If you were there, you might be tempted to glance upwards, once in a while, as if expecting to find some royal figures in full regalia looking down on you from the balconies. We are fond of superlatives. Once we get hold of an idea, we want to stretch it to its outer limits. Nothing short of that will do. The setting had extravagance written all over its expanse.

The marquee was pitched to cover the entire park area across the street from the bride's family home. The set lent a joyous atmosphere to the festive occasion for which it was erected. With a slight stretch of imagination, you could call the function a circus; maybe not literally but no less either. Wait and see.

When the city of New Delhi was planned, they had thrown in a fair amount of a sprinkling of tiny parks in the suburbia. These parkettes are really spots where anything or nothing may grow as determined by the elements as well as the pedestrians and the children who use them as play grounds. This particular park like so many others in the city was a relatively bald spot with practically no vegetation to flaunt. There was an odd stunted tree that had survived the onslaught of the elements and the playfulness of the children of the neighbourhood thus disallowing you to call the park entirely bereft of vegetation.

Another salient feature of Delhi, as of any other big city in India, is its vast population of those who have come to be known as the *jhuggi-jhonpri* dwellers. Jhuggies or jhonpries are huts built with materials collected from here, there and everywhere. They cover every conceivable spot in the sprawling metropolis in a screaming contrast to the posh colonies of New Delhi and its suburbs. Pieces of tin from broken cans, cardboard from discarded boxes, straw, mud and pieces of wood in all shapes and sizes have been used to build these eyesores. Like parasites, these dwellings cling to every inch of space they can hold on to. If you have been to a shanty town in America, you will know what jhuggi-jhonpries are. Our jhuggies will match, with credit, anything that a shanty town may want to throw at them in terms of alcoholics, drug addicts or petty criminals per capita. Our jhuggies have more cell phones and colour TVs per family than the most posh slum in the USA. We do not have as many homeless individuals, though. Family system has shown great tenacity and has survived even among the most destitute. In fact the strength of family ties in India is inversely proportionate to the worth of the worldly possessions of the families concerned.

Ever expanding, these jhuggi-jhonpri colonies know no zoning laws. In fact, these urban ulcerations, with their stench and squalor, are nonexistent to the record keepers of the Municipal Corporation. Keeping a tag on this section of humanity would be as difficult as accounting individually for each one of the crawling worms in festering wounds, worms especially fond of travelling, within their limits of course. The residents of these colonies are collectively the multitudes affectionately known to the politicians as the vote bank. Short on everything that the good Lord provides for His creation, they are big in numbers.

The political fortunes of Mr. Alok K. Sood, whose daughter is getting married today, soar in direct proportion to the swell in these numbers. In return Mr. Sood takes great pains in convincing the residents of these shanties that their welfare is his main concern in life.

As a matter of convenience (to the marriage party, not the general traffic) the street has been blocked off to the public. A canopy has been stretched to cover this section of the street creating a corridor between the block of prosperous looking homes and the gigantic tent. The children who normally occupy the park in the afternoons and the evenings to play cricket, having been temporarily dispossessed of their facilities, have moved to the streets on the other sides of the park where organized games of any sort are impossible due to the volume of traffic.

I am a pushover for unwanted invitations. While wild horses won't be able to drag a sensible man to the funeral of a distant relative whom he had never seen alive, you will find me standing in the front row dressed in a shiny black suit.

I whispered into the left ear of the lady mourner seated beside me, in one such situation. (At least one of us would have to be a contortionist to enlist the services of her right ear because, as it happened, in the colour scheme of the funeral home where dead bodies are entertained, she was arranged to my right.)

"What was the name, God rest him in peace?" Making my face miserable, I inquired of the lady in mourning, squeezing as much sweetness and sympathy into my voice as one can in a whisper.

"Mrs. Brown was my mother." Wide eyed, she hissed back through clenched teeth with unreserved display of shock and disbelief.

But that was then and this is now. I knew no one from either of the two families, neither the Vermas nor the Soods. If every member of these two clans were sitting on their individual mountain of coins, not the most considerate among them would give me change for a rupee. I know their kind. My presence in these alien environs could not be accounted for by any sense of common bonding. Instead, I was there because somebody from my family had to be there, as is required by the, as yet unwritten, code of social conduct. That at least is what my distant nephew, Ramesh, the one who had dragged me into this mess and one of whose army of best friends it was who was getting hitched tonight, would have me believe.

Ramesh and I are almost the same age. We had grown up together and have always been good friends. But we are poles apart as persons. Ramesh is dashing and worldly-wise with loads of personality. He is a handsome charmer. Everything about him is flashy; he is used to having his way with people. Against him I am a simpleton who can be conned by a ten year old child. Nobody except my mother, may God rest her in peace, had any illusions about my looks. She called me her 'Laal' even though I have no admixture of red pigmentation in my brown complexion. Perhaps she meant I was her 'la'al' (ruby) implying that I was precious to her. I would not dare to differ with her on that point. She addressed me as her Chand because it is beautiful and unlike in English, in Indian languages the moon is a male. The list of the wonderful names she called me is almost inexhaustible.

In our extended family tradition, Ramesh addresses me as uncle despite our age parity. Another reason why I was present in these environs was that my still-as-distant nephew could not find a softer target; not in my family, especially because it resides in the cold climes of far off lands. And if I had kept my schedule, I would now be vacationing in some magic spot of this multifaceted land. All the same, if it were not for the likes of me, they could never manage to get hordes of humanity assembled for vulgarities like this.

I was in my native country but despite my best efforts to mingle and merge I could not relate to my surroundings with a sense of belongingness. Instead I viewed the goings on around me with a sympathetic, even indulgent attitude. I could not position myself as a constituent of the chaotic world around me. At no point in time, since my arrival in this ancient land did I feel that I was in step with the flow of life around me. There was never a moment when I was not conscious of struggling against the thrust of the current. The best I could do was to stand still like a detached observer. I could never tune my thoughts to the Indian notes nor could I be swayed by the rhythmic flow of what seemed to me a series of chaotic renditions of abnormality.

I was reminded of Liz, the beautiful waitress in picturesque Bar Harbour in the US of A. I could easily relate to her feelings when she told me her little story. I had been vacationing in the New England states. She had noticed the license plate on my small convertible sports car and had observed:

"Ah, you are from Nova Scotia, that beautiful spot under the sun."

And she went on to describe how tempted by its warmer climate she had once moved south to Florida. She was ecstatic in her new surroundings. She had no problem finding a comparable job in a restaurant. The beaches were simply heavenly. During the fall nothing changed much. There were no maple leaves turning yellow and then vermilion, setting the countryside ablaze. She still stood her ground. But then it was the middle of winter and still nothing seemed to change. She felt uneasy to begin with but slowly but surely she started going crazy. She knew what it was. She was conditioned to seeing dramatic change of seasons. She particularly missed snow. She was a fish out of water. She picked up her bags and took a flight back home. Vacationing was fine but no way could she live in Florida.

The marriage party, the friends and relatives of the groom, of whom I was a part walked behind the noisy band as we marched toward the mother of all tents. People who had nothing better to do crowded the street on both sides of the procession looking at the slowly advancing marriage party with the same spirit as is exhibited by children as they walk past the cages in a zoo. People were gathered even in the upper floor balconies of their homes. Some were perched on roof tops. It seemed that the entire population along the street had come out to watch the procession. Those whose homes were not on this street had come to their neighbours' homes. This was not the kind of show they would want to miss.

There were shirtless, barefoot, filthy street children with grimy faces, unkempt hair and mouths agape exhibiting a total lack of self consciousness. They stared with blank eyes. One urchin came a bit too close to me making me feel uncomfortable. He was darker than the rest of the gang. Like most of his companions he had sunken cheeks and high cheek bones. The only piece of clothing he had on, like the rest of them, was a loose pair of boxer shorts. His ribs were sticking out from under the stretched skin. You could wrap your fingers around his collar bones; they were jutting so far out. With a skeletal torso and spindly arms and legs he had an emaciated, famished look. But in spite of his general state of health he was lively and his eyes sparkled with mischief. The grinning shock-headed rascal looked like he would pull my pants down if I took my eyes off him. The leering twitch on his face gave me the shivers. He had such a ghost like appearance; I squirmed and put another one from the party between the Rascal and me.

The earth seemed to shake with the noise of the ear-splitting band. It was hurting the ear-drums. I slowed down to put as much distance between the deafening band and me as was possible without missing the party. As such I was happy to bring up the fag-end of the entourage. If you were keen on pointing out something louder than the band, it would have to be the bright red and blue colours of the shiny uniforms of the dark skinned band members. The clarinet player who obviously was the band master distinguished himself by being the only one of the band who was not wearing the uniform. He was casually dressed.

The male dominated marriage party included some young girls. Marriage parties in northern India used to be all male affairs until recently. Inclusion of women, comprising mostly young marriageable girls, is a recent phenomenon. These girls are generally given expensive makeovers for the occasion in the hope that they shall be noticed by the eligible bachelor men and their parents. The girls try to put their best foot forward as they dance along young men of the party.

The band is really noisy. The dancers are twisting and turning as they make slow progress towards the tent. Sometimes one of them would interrupt his dance to try to pull some unwilling member of the party to join the circle of dancers. The band led us to the entrance of the tent where we were greeted by the bride's family who stood there with flower garlands in their hands. One by one we were introduced to the parents of the bride.

When it was my turn Ramesh presented me to the St. Bernard drooping eyes and the triple chin poised above a mass of unspecified tonnage which I assumed would be Mrs. Sood, mother of the bride. You could have opened your own half decent independent jewellery business with what the lady was wearing by way of embellishment.

"Auntie, this is my uncle Dave from Canada," said Ramesh pronouncing it as Dave as if it were a Christian name, and not as Dev, the Indian version.

"I am so glad to meet you, Dave," cooed the moon-face sending a ripple through the chins.

"Likewise, I'm sure," I said.

"I have heard Canada described as the most wonderful country in the world. Is it really as beautiful as they say it is?" asked Mrs. Sood.

"It is a beautiful country inhabited by beautiful people."

I moved on. I had no desire to make new friends; instead I wanted to lose myself in the crowd. I did not feel like exchanging views with anyone. I felt rather lonely, surrounded by total strangers in equally strange environs.

All this while the band-sans-music blared in the corner creating a din that hurt the ears. The band seemed to be attempting at striking some semblance between some popular Indian film tunes and what they were playing. They were failing miserably. Those playing the wind instruments were visibly out of breath and were gasping with mouths open wide between short intervals of striking notes. Imagine fish out of water and you will get the picture.

There were chairs arranged in rows on one side of the enclosure. I took a back seat. I shook my head in a bid to shoo away the boredom that was waiting in the aisle, as it were, well poised and itching to move in. If you are a westerner it may interest you to know that basically there are two seasons in the plains of India; hot and hotter. It was hotter and I was perspiring profusely under the collar. I lifted my left arm slightly and smelled. “I stink therefore I am,” I mused mischievously. That was when a young man approached me and introduced himself as Jagat, better known as Jagga. His well oiled hair, parted in the middle, was plastered to his skull. If his eyes were any closer to each other, they would have to be planted on his snub sneezing apparatus. As if resentful of its own existence, his nose almost succeeded in burying itself under the surface. A face-first fall to the ground would give a statue the same look if the accident happened before the plaster-of-paris had had a chance to harden. To give a finishing touch to the picture he sported a thin line of a moustache with a slight interruption in the middle. He was wearing a freshly pressed maroon suit with a ready made bright yellow bow tie at a slant. An assortment of rings adorned his fingers. His shoes were jutting out and upward in front in a pointed finish a few inches beyond the reach of his toes. You might be tempted to think that he would be in his element carrying his individual banner in a gay rights march.

"Please let me know if you need anything, sir. I am at your service. I am a loyal servant of this family," he informed me and I thanked him for being so considerate. He had a habit of smoothing his already smooth shiny hair in a self-conscious manner as he spoke while shuffling his feet; something comparable to girls that keep pushing back their tresses.

Jagga had a strong smell of liquor on his breath. He had a rather engaging manner. In the next couple of minutes he tried to impress me with his importance as the vote bank agent. He would have me believe that he was the kingpin on which the political edifice of Mr Sood's career rested. At the sight of Mrs. Sood approaching, he eased himself out of the picture.

"Ha! There you are," Having been through and done with her duties at the reception, the 'Auntie' accosted me again.

"This band is so noisy," she frowned.

"Pity. They don't come with volume control," I tried to cheer her.

Mrs. Sood was accompanied by a skinny young girl with high cheek bones and prominent upper front teeth.

"This is Naina, my younger daughter," beamed Mrs. Sood as champions do when they hold their trophy high for all to witness. She was trying to speak above the babble of voices around. Meena is the one getting married today, according to the invitation card.

"How are you Naina?" I greeted the girl.

"Hi," Said Naina.

How inappropriate her name was, I pondered. 'Naina' is the Indian word for 'eyes'. Unlike most Indian girls who have beautiful eyes, there was nothing striking about Naina's *naina.* Her name should have been Danta, I pondered mischievously. ('Dant' is Indian for 'teeth'.) If Naina had only thirty two teeth, and I have my serious doubts on the subject, they were all arrayed in almost a straight line behind her wide mouthed lips, engaged in a relentless struggle to keep them apart. As a result, despite her best efforts she could not completely close her mouth.

"Are you having a good time?" asked Mrs. Sood.

"I'm OK." I stifled a yawn as I spoke.

"Surely you are not getting bored?" She was being very nice, considering that she was a stranger a while ago and was going to be a stranger again after tonight.

"Not at all, I'm fine." I lied.

"You are not drinking anything. Have something to drink. What will you have, Scotch?"

While she was talking to me, she looked around and got the attention of one of the waiters who were busy serving drinks. The waiter held the tray in front of me. There were the mixed alcoholic drinks and a few pop bottles.

"A coke should do." I picked one up.

"Surely Dave, you can do better than that. Whisky in Canada, they say, is cheaper than water," said Mrs. Sood.

"That is not true, madam." I was being unnecessarily apologetic about it.

"You don't have to be so formal, Dave. You can call me 'Auntie' as Ramesh does. I am sorry but I have to leave. I have to look after some guests. Naina, make sure Dave feels at home," she instructed the girl.

"You know, we are quite informal with our friends," she assured me as she parted with a meaningful smile on her face.

"Dave, what do you do in Canada?" Naina wanted to know after her mother's departure.

"Oh, this and that," I said inattentively. "Do you have any idea where I can get hold of Ramesh?"

"It would be hard to keep track of Ramesh in a place full of young girls." She said with evident relish.

"You must have a few girl friends of your own in Canada," she added after a pause.

"There are a few ladies among my friends, but none that would fit the role of a girl friend." I tried to set the records straight.

Mrs. Sood came back to check on us. "Are you two having a good time?" she inquired.

"Naina is being very kind to me," I said.

"After Canada, you must find life in India quite dull," said Mrs. Sood.

"On the contrary, I find it very fascinating," I assured her.

"What keeps you busy in Canada, Dave?" She seemed to be in league with her daughter on this issue.

"There is always something to do. It doesn't take much to keep me busy."

"Nobody has to earn money in Canada, I have heard, they just rake it in." She laughed as she made this remark.

"That's a good one," I said.

"How do you spend your time in Canada?" she insisted on knowing.

"Wielding my tiny rake," I said evasively.

"I mean, what you do for a living." she was bent upon getting the information even if she had to squeeze it out of me. I am no high priest of letters but I make a half decent living in the literary world.

"I sell shoes." I decided that I couldn’t deny myself some fun.

"Shoes?" She found it hard to believe that any sensible person should be engaged thus.

"Used shoes," I threw in the last straw.

"Used shoes?" interjected Naina, providing a breather for her mother who was trying to recover from the shock.

"You mean you sell second hand shoes?" asked the wide eyed girl in disbelief.

"They would be more like second foot shoes, won't they?" I said, trying not to leave any room for confusion.

"From where do you get your used shoes?" This was an expression of contempt more than a serious inquiry.

"Somehow they would have to come from first foot users, one would imagine," I filled in.

Suddenly Mrs. Sood assumed the appearance like she had just swallowed a sandstorm and she gave me the look that read, "What the hell are you doing HERE?"

For once I found myself in perfect sync with her line of reasoning. What, in the name of whatever was sacred to either one of us, was I doing there?

"There is not much money in used shoes, though," I said apologetically, hoping this would finally put a lid on the issue of my 'financial misfortune'.

As soon as the ladies departed I left my seat and decided that I would be better off on my feet. With no sense of any particular direction, I went around avoiding the densest section of the gathering and avoiding any eye contact.

The bridegroom, the scion of the Verma family, was in the light-heavy weight division of tycoonery, a new star on the industrial horizon of India, who had bulldozed his way into the dog-eat-dog business world of modern India.

The hullabaloo was staged to unite, in holy matrimony, the Vermas with the Sood family that had recently emerged on the capital's cutthroat (the use of the term is not symbolic) political arena.

If you are familiar with the lives of the elite of the business world in India, you know that marriages here, in the style of the globally touted Chrysler-Mercedes sleeping arrangements, serve a much wider purpose than the union of two persons in wedlock. Marriages are generally arranged more to serve the extended financial and political interests of the families concerned than to safeguard the rather limited stakes of the couple. It would be no misstatement to say that in the higher echelons of society in India, the stock market has replaced heaven as the venue where marriages are arranged.

Under the majestic dome of this gigantic tent, this here was a much larger assembly of tuxedos than you can expect to see at a single glance in the most populous rookery of penguins south of the Antarctic Circle.

The rustle of silk saris on female figures, with the exposed midriff, was reminiscent of the whisper of breeze blowing through the tall strands of the prairie grasslands. There was a generous and indiscriminate use of perfume, with a blatant disregard for the notions of 'his' and 'hers'. The scent floated way ahead of the wearers. There was nothing in the entire set up that would owe its indebtedness to words like subtle, mellow or modest: A vulgar display of sheer affluence without any admixture of taste.

The nerve racking and seemingly never ending wedding ceremony having come to a close at last, the bride and the bridegroom were escorted up a stage on one end of the arena. The stage was covered with a luxurious Persian carpet and matching twin maroon velvet, gold brocaded thrones with expensive looking carvings and gold trimmings were in place.

If you did not know that all that glittered was not gold, you might be led to believe that during the heyday of the British Raj these thickly cushioned thrones caressed and supported the equally generously cushioned regal derrieres of some nawab and his begum or a maharaja and his maharani in the capital of a protectorate princely state, under the patronizing but watchful eye of the British consul.

Our obese maharaja and his dud maharani having been planted in the thrones, Their Majesties' loyal subjects, the entire concourse, fortuitously placed together by destiny, now started to form into what might pass as a semblance of a queue. I had been through such routines before, never on this scale of vulgarity, though. It came to me as no surprise that no one was pushing or shoving to move ahead. Instead, overly polite, everyone seemed to be yielding to everyone else. They knew their exact place in this class conscious assemblage. There are classes within classes.

Ramesh spotted me. Dancing his way in and out through the thicket of the crowd, he came and led me lightly by the arm and placed me in the queue where, if I could hold that position at the finish of a marathon race, though I would not be dreaming of holding the trophy aloft and smiling to the cameras, I would certainly win an honourable mention. This was, what you might call, the pay-up time.

We do not normally bring gifts to the weddings. Nothing short of hard cash will do. And in the queue, the vantage positions are taken up by the bigger donors or so it seems.

One person at a time, friends, relatives, business associates, business rivals and non-of-the-above inched up to the backs of the thrones. Exposed to the piercing stares of the multitudes and in full view of the dozen or so cameras with movie lights and popping flash lights, each lined up person took out bills of large denomination from where they had been kept in readiness. On reaching the thrones they would wave the money in circles over and around the heads of the newly weds, as if tracing halos, and would place it lightly on the piling mountains of currency in the laps of the couple.

That distant relative's polite nudge had placed me in the category of a couple of a thousand rupee bills. The English language has never been subjected to express the kinds of thoughts that rang through my head as I parted company with those crisp pieces of paper. If only that pseudo-nephew of mine, the subject of my wild imagination, could decipher and record the goings on in my mind, he would have a fairly sound case to take me to court for indulging in libellous obscenities. In the bargain he would have learnt a thing or two about parts of his anatomy. I muttered a string of expletives that were miserably inadequate to express my feelings.

The revenues having been collected, the bundles of loot having been passed on to the custodians of the bridegroom's family, the couple descended from the thrones and walked toward the centre of the arena. The band having been given a break, a *dhol* player started beating his drum with a fury that knew no tomorrow. As if a switch had been pressed, the formally dressed crowd broke into a frenzy of dance hysteria, oblivious of the world beyond the dancing floor, of the fact that their steps that night were in rhythm with the guns spouting death in Doda, in Kashmir, what was once Heaven on Earth; oblivious of the disco lights above them being in sync with the mortar flashes in Guwahati in the Northeast. Dancing mostly above the waist, they were waving their arms frantically heavenwards as if they were drowning.

And at the heart of this rumpus, the bridegroom's father, walking behind the couple, marched into centre-court. He held fresh rolls of one thousand rupee bills in his hand, With an elaborate flourish, he pulled a handful from the wad and holding them above the heads of the couple, like one spreads playing cards in one's hand, for all and sundry to witness, he flung the cash into the air.

It was raining thousand rupee bills. Another roll came out and yet another. On and on it went, a seemingly unending shower of cash. It would seem that the man had finally decided to rid himself of his materialistic attachments and give everything away in "charity." It appeared that he was going to say good bye to the phenomenal world right after he finishes his last act of generosity and that the man would walk out of this place and head straight for a cave in the Himalayas. He was determined that his largesse would remain unmatched since the eras of the legendary Maharaja Harish Chander and that of Hatim Tai.

On closer scrutiny, however, one could see that the ring of young men of the clan around the newlyweds was impregnable. The tuxedo clad boys were busy snatching up the bills before they could hit the ground. Every bill was being returned to the bridegroom's older brother. Each bill was accounted for and returned to its source.

While this drama was being enacted under the high dome, oblivious of the game plan and lured by the love of mammon, some smelly, sweaty, bare-chested, street urchins, products of the festering slums of the neighbourhood, mistook the farce for reality. They trespassed into the tent but stayed huddled together near the entrance as if to muster enough courage to venture into what seemed like the war zone.

All boys, almost all of them wore just one piece of clothing, something that had the semblance of long underpants or boxer shorts. All were barefoot and most were shirtless. They were promptly chased out by some swearing, drunken young men from the marriage party. The screaming little devils ran for the safety of the world outside.

All seemed to be quiet on that front until two little wretches, unnoticed by the bacchanalia, ventured to infiltrate into the field of action. About nine or ten years of age, these daredevils sneaked from under the wall of the tent closest to the raining money. Overawed by their surroundings, they froze in their tracks immediately after entry. Sense of mutual support, if any, had dissipated. Starry eyed, mouths open, they stood petrified. Tiny and frail, and yet they were conspicuous, like ugly warts.

The ominous moment seemed to hang an eternity and then it was the scene of a feeding frenzy in a pool of sharks. The children were grabbed and fists started flying while the show of the showering money went on uninterrupted. One of the children was lucky to escape with minor injuries as he made a dash for the safety beyond the walls of the tent.

The back of the other was towards me. I shall never forget the tear in his shorts where it mattered most. One zealous defender of the social bastion, the one who had been introduced to me as Ganesh, heaved a massive uppercut, as if lifting it from the ground, and brought it to impact the solar plexus of the tot that lifted him off his feet. Once more he struck him.

The kid was lying face down when I approached him. As I tried to turn him over, he sprang up, took a step, fell again, got up and ran out of the tent. Perhaps fear gave him the energy or may be an instinctive reflex gave him the push. He was the ‘Rascal’, as I had known him.

I had a feeling of sickness in my stomach. Not knowing what I was up to, I walked out into the familiar Delhi street scene of a late evening; the heat, the humidity, the stench, the choking anger and the faceless multitudes.

At no place on earth, outside of South Asia, will you find such variety or such density of traffic. The tricycle pedal rickshaws, the tricycle motorized taxi scooters popularly known as the three wheelers, weaving through the rubble of humanity--- and the bicycles: The oddity about the bicycles is that the rider sits so high that at a stand still he cannot rest his toes on the ground. So he has to dismount and mount at every stop by swinging his leg over the back of the contraption; and they can manage to do it in such a congested, mingled mass of man and machine.

The hand drawn cargo carriages and the horse pulled tongas are not to be left behind: The lines of donkeys with the twin bags evenly balanced over their backs with their loads of bricks. There is even an odd camel drawn cart. The buses, known locally as the Killer Line, can race through this maze at speeds one would not dare attempt on deserted roads; this though not without its toll of human life. That is why the name. But human life here is an expendable commodity. Everybody seems to be speeding from somewhere to somewhere with the frenzy matched only at an ant hill. And having reached wherever they are going, one simply marvels, some of them can sit motionless, staring vacantly into space; expert at doing nothing.

The scared look of the 'Rascal' had singed my soul like the red hot iron marks the rump of a heifer. Tears rolled down my cheeks as I wandered aimlessly about. I was possessed by a maddening urge to grab this distorted, twisted world along with its obese aunties and their puffed up litters by the neck and wrench the life out of it. Only I did not know how to go about it. I felt so impotent. I would have cried out aloud or committed some other crazy act if only I had the courage.

In front of the cluster of huts, all covered with multicoloured rags, there was a knot of dark skinned men and women. Instinctively my feet dragged me to it. Some of the women were sobbing. The crowd made way for me as I approached. A woman sat on the ground waving her arms over her head in desperation. A man in his forties, old and wrinkled, was trying to pacify her. The nucleus of this sober gathering was the body of the child whose face is etched on my mind for eternity. Dishevelled hair clinging to his face, he lay there peacefully amid this commotion. It was the 'Rascal'.

"You can't do better than that," Jagga was saying to the man who was trying to calm the hysterical woman.

"Your son is not coming back. And you are not the only one who has been hurt. It is a very bad omen for the wedding, you know? And you cannot say they are not trying to share your misfortune. If you ask me, they are being very generous about it. And what else can you do? Surely you cannot take them to court. That needs a lot of money. I have already spoken to the police. They say there is no case. Nobody seems to have seen anything. There are no witnesses ready to come forward. Ramlal, we are like fish in the river, we cannot afford to antagonize the crocodiles," Jagga pleaded with the father of the dead boy.

With an elaborate flourish, he took out of his pocket two five hundred rupee bills and stuffed them into the breast pocket of Ramlal's shirt.

"And this is not all; I am going to insist that they pay for the cremation too. I am not going to let them off the hook easily," Jagga spoke with emphasis, in a final bid to clinch the deal for his masters.

The young men were still protesting. One of them said something about the value of human life. A thousand rupees cannot bring back their son, he argued.

Exhibiting frustration, this time Jagga addressed the most vocal of the young men:

"And what do you suggest they should do to bring back their son? What option do they have? I have already done my own investigation. There are no witnesses. For all practical purposes no crime has been committed. Courts go by eyewitness accounts. In this case there is no eyewitness. Nobody saw anything."

"I did." Somewhere inside me a safety valve burst open. Face distorted with rage, I heard myself shouting. "I did." My yell rang through the neighbourhood. This was the celebration shout of a victor who has thrust the sword home.

There was pin-drop silence. The wailing, the moaning, the bickering, the arguments came to a sudden halt. As if struck by lightening, Jagga stood there with shock and disbelief writ large on his face. His lower jaw hanging down, he stared at me with incredulous eyes.

The crowd sensed the import of my outburst. It sounded like a death-knell. Ganesh's goose, it seemed, was cooked. Jagga's own position was untenable. He had been bribing the bereaved family, trying to buy impunity from justice for his masters. With visible relief and some degree of elation as was possible under the circumstances, the mourners seemed to welcome my presence.

For the first time since I landed in this blessed land of my ancestors, this evening I felt like I had my feet on solid ground. Now I was absolutely sure of myself. I was on very sound footing and I knew what I was up to: You miserable, twisted world, get ready to swing because for once I have got you by the balls.

*****

The Money Order

After a couple of centuries of humiliation, the Ganga finally shed the "Ganges" shroud thrown over her by British Imperialism and bade farewell to a caricatured identity that was conferred on her by the alien conquerors to fig-leaf her shame of slavery. The Ganga has reclaimed her nativity that had sanctified her through the millennia. Bathed in the aura of her pristine glory, she surges and heaves suckling the vast planes of northern India.

The aorta of body India, she bestows life and vitality as she pulsates through the heartland of this eternal nation. Like the devoted mother that she is, Ganga *Maiya* (Mother Ganga) endeavours to keep her children clean, polluting herself in the process. She transports the hazardous industrial waste and the personal dirt of billions of humans and animals to the Bay of Bengal, complimenting in her own humble way the much larger contribution of the polluted rivers of the industrialized nations of the world. In the manner of an intricate circulatory system, the Ganga is assisted in her immense task by hundreds of tributaries traversing the vast plains of northern India.

On this hot and humid sunny afternoon, on one of the smaller tributaries of the Ganga, with her burden of various wares, a barge floats slowly downstream. Reflective of its tranquil surroundings, unmindful of time, like an elephant heavy with her calf she moves on the unhurried waters of the river that slithers through the lush green plain like a giant serpent. The barge appears to be caught up in the stillness of the landscape: The kind of stillness that would engulf heaven and earth. It hung heavy as it descended upon every blade in the paddy fields. There was not the slightest hint of wind; Frozen in time, nature seemed to be holding its breath. All was still; stirred not a leaf. The silence was so profound you could hear it echo around you. It was the kind of a deafening quietude that you could have sliced and doled out to those stricken with noise pollution rendering much needed relief. On the other hand it had the potential of invading the unsuspecting susceptibilities of a city-dweller from a mile away, driving him nuts. But then, you might want to know, what would the unsuspecting susceptibilities of a city-dweller be doing a mile away from an alien environ such as this where they wouldn't be caught dead. What, indeed?

The multipurpose barge on this tributary of the Ganga, apart from transporting people and goods, served as a floating post office for the hamlets sprinkled along the banks of the river. The cargo included boxes, bundles in all shapes and sizes; large, shallow baskets stuffed with live chickens, held down with nets, their heads sticking out through the holes as if they were trying to sprout out of themselves. There were even a goat and a couple of pigs tied in a corner.

The barge skirted at a distance the almost denuded tree which with its rotting roots submerged in the slow moving water looked deader than death; driftwood that refused to drift. But in this skeletal frame of mostly dry wood life was sustained in the barest hint of chlorophyll preserved in the microscopic tuft of foliage at the very end of the topmost branch. Somehow this caricature, of what in an age gone by, before the onslaught of the changing course of the river, must have been a magnificent tree, was holding on to dear life by a prayer like the withered old man who ravaged by time and disease is reduced to a skeleton but refuses to call it a day and in a dignified manner kick the bucket, spare the space and move on.

There was hardly any activity on the barge that was floating downstream, except a couple of bare-foot, bare-chested, brown-skinned men in white loincloths walking back and forth along either edge of the deck, steering and nudging the boat along with long bamboo poles thrust deep into the soft river bed, keeping it midstream where the water is deep and the current relatively strong. The dozen or so passengers were scattered on the deck under the canopy in reclining or lying postures. The elderly postmaster who doubled as a mailman, exhausted by heat and humidity was prostrate on his wooden settee. With a small towel in one hand he was wiping the perspiration off his face and neck repeatedly. With the other hand he was trying to fan himself with a straw fan but was finding the exercise too exacting.

Amidst the paddy fields and a fair scattering of mango trees, Balighat, the drowsy hamlet baked in the sun. Balighat is a bunch of a score or so mud huts with thatched roofs, arranged to follow the contours of the landscape along a single winding street of varying width and elevation. The village had not yet been introduced to a baked brick.

In the shade of a centuries old banyan tree, in front of his little hut, a diminutive wizened old man, oblivious of and neglected by the world around him, was sitting on his feet, his arms folded in front and resting on his knees, caught in a cataleptic quietude as if planted there and forgotten by time. South Asians are the only people on earth who can sit for hours on their feet, like a hen ready to lay an egg giving you the impression that this is the most comfortable posture to relax in.

Chandu, the old man was only in his early fifties but these years had played havoc with this micro sample of humanity. In terms of the extent and harshness of disease, hunger and back breaking labour that was packed into it, the past half century could be stretched into an eternity. Like you can determine the age of a tree by counting the rings in its trunk, you could count the fifty odd years in the deeply etched wrinkles furrowed on his face. But you wouldn't want to waste your time on such a fruitless exercise.

Perhaps the most striking feature of the old man's person, if anything relating to his person could be thus described, was his aquiline nose. The tip of the smooth, even, protruding curve of the nose gave a philosophic observer the impression that it was in its own silent way expressing a deep rooted longing to meet his chin, going more than half way over to bridge the gap across his unimposing mouth. One would, in all fairness, expect some reciprocal effort on the part of the chin to rise to the occasion and say 'hello' but there was no red carpet, not even a welcome sign hanging out there simply because there was no chin on location. The jowl terminus was there alright but the chin was absent from its post. Rather unfair considering that some people have more than their share of these protuberances. The front end of the lower jaw seemed to slope hurriedly backward and downward to meet the neck. If there was a rule that drooping bowline noses are to be matched with equally jutting curved-up chins then Chandu was the nature's exception intended to prove the rule.

Because of some quite logical and as yet unresolved differences between them, Chandu's beady eyes, at the risk of falling off his face, tried to put as much distance between them as the ground realities would permit. Any farther apart and they would have gone overboard or would have to be pasted to the temples on the sides of his face like those of an iguana.

It was so quiet that Chandu could have heard the young widow's occasional sigh next door, if only he were paying attention. Godavri was a widow at twenty two. She had been married to Ramdhan, a young man from Pulona, a neighboring village. Ramdhan used to peddle a rented tricycle rickshaw in a small town forty five kilometers from Balighat, Godavri's native village. He would leave her before daybreak and come back home late at night. He was working hard, he explained to Godavri, to save enough money to be able to buy their own rickshaw and a shanty one day instead of renting one as they did now. After all there were going to be additions to the family in the days to come.

They were planning on having two children, a boy and a girl but no more. But they were not going to have any children until they had their own rickshaw and their very own shanty. Godavri had a lighter skin than most other women of the area. She was very likeable and the couple were quite comfortable with their neighbors. Godavri lived happily with Ramdhan in the slum area of the small town for about seven months until one day people brought Ramdhan's dead body to her. His rickshaw had been hit by a speeding bus. Ramdhan had died on the spot. Godavri was forced to come back to her native village to live with her widowed father and with shattered dreams buried in her bosom. Here she settled down to the monotony of a peaceful life of mourning, living and reliving her memories of the ecstatic nights spent in the arms of Ramdhan. She resigned herself to her destiny in which her sole social encounter would be with her father with whom she exchanged a few words everyday. Her father would come home only for his meals and to sleep. The rest of the time he was either working in his fields or socializing with his friends. He was very fond of his daughter and felt sorry for her but there was not much he could do for her.

At the sight of the barge, Chandu simply refused to stay blended in the tranquillity of the scene. He got up in a hurry and scurried along through the steaming lush green paddy fields, following a narrow winding pathway toward the landing. But before long, exhausted by the sudden burst of his pace, he settled down to a more comfortable gait toward the moorings.

His dangling genitalia, profiled magnificently in the sunlight was frame-bracketed by his bow legs as it swung rhythmically in his diaphanous loincloth. Why is this not-quite-so-far-out-of-the-ordinary phenomenon considered mentionable? Is there something unique about it? The answer is "Yes" and "No". Here is why:

There is nothing singularly trend-setting or epoch-making about the genitals (Chandu's or his second cousin's, for that matter, that is, if he had a second cousin and also if his second cousin did not wear a sari.) being on display in this manner. It is a fashion statement quite in vogue among the translucent muslin (the world famous muslin so fine that a whole roll may be pulled through a finger ring) loincloth donning males of this region and is comparable to the bosom flaunting instinct of the females of the species. What is unique is not the manner, but the mass of the object on display, 'exhibit A', as a legal mind would put it.

You have seen the public sector industrial undertakings in this blessed country; the sprawling enterprises that pock-mark the vast land; imposing in size but short on production. Similar was the case of Chandu's twin testosterone plants, supposedly producing sperms; compared to the mass of the units, the meagre output that never had a chance to get put out was nothing to write home about. To make things simple, it may be stated in all sincerity that innocent people had at times thought, erroneously, of course, that Chandu was carrying his grocery bag under his loincloth: An honest mistake, given the circumstance and the unshakeable, swingable evidence in danglestance. It was a case of *dangleosis magnifique* or, in medicos' lingo, 'hydrocele' of the elephantine persuasion.

And no one, not even those who knew him intimately, which included practically everybody in the neighbourhood, could say with absolute certainty that since 'exhibit A' started gathering its extra mass and prominence Chandu's bow legs had not arched further out, gravity taking its toll and playing its assigned role, as we know it.

When we walk it is natural to swing our arms. When we walk faster we swing them faster and farther out. If you were told to walk without swinging your arms, it would not only be inconvenient, it would take more energy. Chandu was no biophysicist but he had learnt this truth and had learnt to apply it successfully to his advantage. When you have a lemon, you learn to make lemonade. Chandu had likewise learnt to create, as he walked, a rhythmic swing in the backward and forward movement of the 'grocery bag', the object under our observation, coupled with a bobbing forward movement of his body. The first time he was able to build a pleasurable rhythmic swing with some degree of finesse he was happier than a little ballerina who has just completed her first unaided spin on her toes.

On his way to the river Chandu broke his rhythm only once. That was when he had spotted a grasshopper directly in the line of his progress. The temptation to jump onto it was too much to pass by. He performed the act with the deftness of a youthful athlete. The mission having been accomplished, he resumed his rhythmic gait.

Having arrived at the landing, he gasped for a good sized breath of heat and humidity and made an effort to adjust himself to a stationary upright position.

The barge was still some distance from the landing when Chandu filled his lungs with air and bellowed in its direction:

"Have you got my money?"

This exercise, in actual fact, was more an expression of his own sense of well being than a serious inquiry relating to his finances. Chandu was expecting no money from any quarters, not yet anyway. His yell was the human version of the cock-a-doodle-do of a proud rooster who acknowledges that the Lord is in His heaven and, with his own harem (the rooster's and not the Lord's) in place; all is well with the world. Our hero, though, never had anything even remotely resembling a harem, not even a single unit one except for a very short spell when he was married to Santhali who had died giving birth to their only child, a boy who having grown up had left his father in search of work.

For the first time in his troubled sojourn on this planet, this middle-aged-old man was experiencing a state of self fulfilling elation. For the best part of his life of toil and tribulation he did not often possess a couple of coins to rub against each other. You might be tempted to argue that even now, financially speaking, he was doing no better than holding on to bare subsistence. All the same he felt that he had attained a certain financial status in his community. He honestly believed that everybody in this neighbourhood of villages was envious of his newly acquired prosperity. He also firmly believed that the more widely known was his state of financial 'abundance' the better it would be in the fitness of things. Thus he was determined to make it absolutely certain that everybody acknowledged his worth.

Having been relieved of the worry of chasing a bare subsistence-level livelihood that had eluded him until the recently acquired inflow of steady cash, he had even started entertaining dreams of hitching up with Godavri, the young widow residing in his immediate neighbourhood.

Having received no answer to his query, Chandu shouted again:

"Have you brought my money yet?"

In the barge, the postmaster-cum-mailman just frowned. Only last week he had delivered the five hundred rupee[1] money order that came but once a month.

As the barge came to the mooring, old Chandu was helped to get on board by one of the bare-chested men. The next landing, a couple of kilometres downstream was Ishapur, the small marketplace of the locality. Chandu got off the barge and took notice of the wooden-boxed tea stall near the landing. It caught his fancy momentarily but he decided against going in. There were not enough people in it. What he needed was an audience. His mind was made up. He headed straight for the sole tavern of the locality. Making himself as conspicuous as possible, he nodded to all and sundry on the way, expecting to elicit salutations in return.

---

[1] Five hundred rupee are roughly equal to nine US dollars.

He sidestepped a little to kick the empty tin can that was lying in the street and sent it bouncing away. Startled by the rattle, the three women who were walking together some distance ahead of him, turned around and looked at him. They were visibly amused by his childish behaviour and responded with suppressed giggles in acknowledgement of the entertaining diversion provided by him. He responded with his own feigned devil-may-care smile. Chandu chased them with his gaze until the jiggling, sniggering trio disappeared around the corner at the intersection.

Chandu had real difficulty in recalling how a mature female body felt against his own pulsating chest; how its quickened breathing felt against his face. It seemed ages since his wife Santhali died. His love life had hopelessly breathed its last along with her. She was buxom and shapely. The master sculptor who had carved the female figures in the Ajanta caves had pretty much Santhali's physique and contours in mind even though Chandu had never heard of Ajanta. All curves, she was built on generous but symmetrical proportions. Her ebony skin was supple and smooth. Shivers went through his spine as he daydreamed of her voluptuous playfulness. No wonder it was his favourite pastime. In the romantic sense his life had since been a desert of unlimited proportions, a vast Sahara that had no outer limits. Dimming memories and an active imagination did not make life any easier in the sexually inhibitive society in which he lived.

In sharp contrast to his late wife, Godavri, the widow in his immediate neighbourhood in the village was slim and comparatively tall. She was sober by nature and had a fair complexion. When in Chandu's presence, which was not often, she always seemed to be gazing on the ground between them. Chandu could not tell with any degree of assurance what the colour of her eyes was. The emptiness in his life was so acute that he yearned for Godavri with his body and soul. But because of his advancing years and the absence of a well wisher to plead his case to Godavri's father there was not much to pin his hopes on.

Thanks to Chandu's antics, he was a popular figure with the regulars at the market's sole watering hole. This tavern was a dark and dingy native version of a hole-in-the-wall saloon. There was only one kind of liquor served here and it was distilled on the premises and brought straight to the customers. You could smell the cheap country liquor if you happened to pass in front of the joint. There was nothing pretentious about this local enterprise. If you wanted a soda to mix with your drink, you would attract attention and stand out like a sore thumb. The 'boy' would have to run across the street to get it for you.

Once inside the premises Chandu was eager to be recognized but had no desire to mix with the regulars. He refused to join the revellers seated on benches on either side of a long table and demanded a separate chair and a stool before he would accept his drink. In deference to his advancing years and his reputation as a crowd pleaser he was given the desired place of honour facing the merry makers.

He took his first sip and before it could trickle down to his gut, for reasons not known even to him he started talking about the irreverent attitude of today's youth. Addressing no one in particular he spoke in the general direction of the assemblage. As the drinks made it to his blood stream, he was aglow with ideas. He waxed eloquent like a seasoned preacher on his best Sunday.

"When we were your age, we lowered our eyes when we addressed an elder. We never dared to look at him."

"Bapu, if you did not look at him, how did you know he was there at all?" interjected a smart one.

"And what is more, we never opened our big mouth until we were told to," Chandu reprimanded.

"Even if you didn't know he wasn't there?" The smart one pushed further, making a serious sniggering face.

Chandu was quite peeved but more than that, unable to make head or tail of the wisecrack, he was confounded. He tried to ignore the interference and to pick up where he had left off but he went blank; in the effort he lost trail of his own drift. He had no idea what he was talking about.

The crowd was enjoying the show. They threw themselves into it wholeheartedly. They were amused by the old man's palaver to begin with but now they were laughing and giggling at his drivel and not too reverentially.

He was overly irritated. His speech became more and more disjointed and fuzzy. Finding the situation slipping out of control, he started behaving like a monarch addressing his rebellious subjects:

"You think life is a joke?" His voice broke as he shouted.

"No Bapu, but you certainly are," someone at the back shouted.

And the merry makers doubled with laughter. Finding the situation getting out of hand and not daring to take on the inebriated bunch, with a drunkard's sharp intuition, he spotted vulnerability. He turned and picked on the boy serving the drinks who also seemed to be having a good time:

"What are you sniggering at you monkey's fart-hole? You find it funny?"

* * *

Fifteen hundred kilometres to the west, Punjab is in turmoil. There is a steady drip of blood and there are echoes of cracking bones. The atmosphere is heavy with the stench of spilled guts. The police blame the militants for the atrocities and the militants accuse the police for the carnage supposedly carried out by the security personal disguised as militants. There is just one indisputable fact; innocent people are dying for no reason at all.

In this reported instance, those killed were mostly men from the east, called *Bhaiyas*[2] in the local lingo. But for them, the economy of Punjab would collapse. With finger nails cracked and dirty, they provide the manpower for the labour intensive agriculture. In the cities they paddle the tricycle rickshaws, transporting people and goods.

There are no Punjabis who are willing to work for the kind of wages, the lure of which brought a flood of migrant workers who left their homes and, in most cases, their families far away in the less prosperous regions of eastern Uttar Pradesh and Bihar, thus stretching out lifelines between the bread winners and the hungry mouths. Hordes of dark, skinny young men and women swarm the countryside, gather at city street intersections waiting to catch the attention of a prospective employer.

That leaves the local youth free to kill; free to be killed. Having come to tame the soil of the wild west, the migrant workers provide cheap labour and, in the context of today's news, cheap blood. The widows in far off homes, for all purposes, remain nonexistent and the orphans unidentified and faceless. There are no statistical figures, because in this grossly overpopulated fledgling democracy such records are deemed unwieldy and superfluous.

This would be the season of joyous colours, of rainbow coloured kites twinkling in the bright sun and of young men crowned with merry bright yellow turbans. Sisters, seeking blessings and protection, would adorn their brothers' turbans with tender new barley shoots. But the brothers are out there, killing, being killed.

The vastness of the fields is devoid of the yellow mustard flower carpets this year. Wheat grows as far as the eye can see. The dark

---

[2] Literally, Brothers.

blotches of blood from where the bodies have been removed seem to punctuate an endless serial tragedy. The day dawns and another sun rises over Punjab, its bloody light oozing through the lifting mist: Drip, drip, drip.

On this fateful day, on a busy highway they stopped a bus and entered. Some, they ordered out of the bus and the rest were told to stay. Everybody knew the fatal import of the selection, but what could anyone do? Some slumped in their seats and some, huddled together, fell in a heap one on another as the AK-47 started spouting death. It was a surgical operation, effortless and smooth, carried out with the precision of professionals. It would, though remain a non-event in so far as the historians are concerned.

The intoxication from the country booze that Chandu was swilling out that day in Ishapur should last him a real long time because among all else, this dithering old man's next money order also got buried in that bloody heap in the bus.

Hurling the blame for the gory executions back and forth, the police and the militants exchanged accusations in the media.

*****

The Quartet

In the grinding wheels of injustice
Tiny buds get crushed:
Stifled sobs and dried up tears
Remain unheard, unnoticed
By the strong and the mighty
Upon whom destiny awaits
That in their own time
They be ground finer.

The women were singing their hearts out. Dressed in flashy colours, they were all young, all four of them. The venue was a wide open courtyard, where cattle would be tied in normal circumstances. It was a rustic setting, the kind you are likely to find in the country outhouse of an average prosperous agriculturist family in Punjab. Along the outer walls of the quadrangle, you could see the long built-in eating troughs for the cattle. The place had been cleaned and sanitized as best as its nature would permit.

The women were singing songs that had been beaten to a pulp by the entertainment media. You could not pass a *paan* shop without being hit by one of these popular Punjabi songs. Like an epidemic they were everywhere; in the cinema, on TV and on the radio. The singers would not exactly fit into the category that a music director on a talent hunt would go crazy about but that did not dampen the gusto of the performers who had never heard of someone called a music director, anyway.

By no stretch of the imagination could you call the light-brown women beautiful, but their youthful vigour and an eagerness to please their clientele more than compensated for any deficiency in the looks department. What made their job a whole lot easier for them was a matching eagerness on the part of the all male audience to be pleased. They were all in a joyous festive mood, bent upon having a good time.

Free liquor provided by the bride's family went a long way in ironing out any wrinkles in the tempers of the elders that might have remained unattended. Some serious cracks in relationships did appear during the long drawn out haggling over the dowry settlement. But all is well, as they say, that ends well. The dowry items were put on display to the mutual satisfaction of all concerned.

The nerve-racking, patience testing, seemingly never ending wedding ceremonies were finally concluded. If anything could have been longer than the speeches of those who were keen on giving unwanted and unheeded advice to the newly wedded couple, it would have to be the faces of the stiff bored non-audience. Everyone heaved a sigh of relief when the tedium finally came to an end.

But all that was over and done now. That was then and this was here and now; the scene of a rural wedding party where expectations from the performers were high.

Jats consider themselves to be the highest caste among the Sikhs. On an average they are easily the tallest and the strongest of all the Indians. Almost all Jats own agricultural land and most of them are professional farmers. Most of those assembled were from well to do Jat Sikh families like the families of the bride and the bridegroom. Then there were those who were from poorer background, relatives all the same. Even these merry makers had scrubbed themselves well behind the ears in preparation for the festive occasion and had donned their select shiny apparel. They had taken great care to get rid of the soil from the fields that was otherwise an indistinguishable, integral part of their being. Some small children from this section of society had pink marks above their upper lips from their runny noses. The children had been cleaned to a shine. These children seemed to be carrying their clothes on their bodies rather than wearing them; they could not relate to their attire with any sense of belongingness. But that did not stop them from flaunting it with visible pride.

Men and boys were scattered all over the yard. Some were occupying creaky squeaky chairs with iron-pipe frames and tin seats arranged around small wooden tables. But most were sitting or reclining in all kinds of imaginable postures on jute-woven cots. There was no order to how things were placed. Before occupying a seat someone would routinely drag his chair to be close to or away from someone or something. Or it could just be an expression of will, of wanting to have things one's own way. The behaviour was normal.

There was one monstrosity of a 'cot' in the arena, placed where the throne would be if this had been the royal court of a princely state during the British Raj instead of the cattle yard in a rustic setting that it was. Going by its measurements, this 'cot' would over-awe a king-size bed. Apart from its size, what gave it the pride of distinction was the fact that it was woven with cotton strip-matting instead of jute string and was covered with white linen. At its head was a huge cylindrical pillow that one can recline against. This *divan* had 'class' written all over it. Occupied and as yet unoccupied chairs were strewn here, there and everywhere.

There was another oddity on the scene. It was this clean shaven man casually dressed in Western style but wearing an Al Capone felt hat. Meaning no disrespect to him, everyone talked of him as '*Topialla*' (man with the hat). But for the manner of his attire and the fact that he was clean shaven he would be indistinguishable from the rest of the crowd. This man had his roots in this part of Punjab but had migrated to Canada in search of greener pastures. He was drawn back to his motherland, as if on the waves of destiny after a shipwreck, and now a sort of a cultural outcast among his own people he found himself parked in one of the chairs removed from the noisier section of the crowd. He was not too far from the 'throne'. And he was facing it. Topialla's father was a petty farmer, a man of meagre means. He had to part with a sizeable chunk of his inherited agricultural land to finance his son's passage abroad. Our man with the hat was lucky to receive a scholarship at Dalhousie University in Halifax and he worked at odd jobs to earn the balance of his expenses.

All through his academic career Topialla (Let us keep calling him that.) had been a straight 'A's student except in one graduate course that he had taken with an Indo-Canadian professor who had awarded him a B+. His response to this award was that of shock and disbelief. There was another student, Naomi, in the same batch who received an A+ for her paper. Naomi was not the brightest of students but she had an exceptionally charming manner and always nestled up to this professor whenever she wanted to get his attention. When it was time to present the term paper she approached our Topialla and asked him with all the sweetness that she could muster, if he would 'help' her with her term paper. Totally disarmed, he could not say no and he ended up writing her entire paper without any contribution from her. Frustrated, at having earned a B+ he confronted the professor. There was no one else within earshot. Quite unabashedly the professor said to him, "Remember you had quarrelled with me once?" What he was alluding to was a tiff they had at a cultural meet totally unrelated to academics or the University.

Topialla was offered a position to teach in the same University after he received his doctorate in English. He welcomed the job and settled in Halifax. Since his emigration this was his first visit to India, the land that he now realized had a billion mysteries buried in her bosom.

Back to the festivities in the yard: Everybody's attention was drawn to the entrance gate as a small procession of some tough looking overfed and under exercised men marched in. They were all gaudily dressed in Punjabi fashion; brightly coloured collarless shirts flowing down well below the knees and strikingly colourful 'bed-sheets' tied around their waists and trailing behind them on the ground. Topping it all, their turbans included all the tints and hues that you can imagine by permuting the various combinations of the colours of a rainbow. If it had not been for the lack of their physical fitness, you would have mistaken them for a *bhangra* dance team. Most of them wore firearms that they were firing into the sky, the old West American style.

At the head of this group was a fright for sore eyes, the fattest man that you ever set your eyes on. The word 'obesity' in any of its grammatical forms would be insufficient to cover his expanse. His ruddy cheeks, symptomatic of a healthy circulatory system or of high blood pressure, flashed like twin suns on the eastern horizon. He was in his early forties but if you had a penetrating eye you would see that this mass of flesh and fat, mostly fat, must have been a well built muscular man not too many years ago. In his younger days he used to boast, with or without justification, that he could tighten the nuts on his car wheels with his bare hand and none is on record for having contradicted him. The insiders knew that these days he wore leather straps on the insides of his thighs to keep them from scraping against each other and becoming sore as he walked, when he walked, which was not too often.

Of course, it is none of our business to know how he 'handled' himself and kept himself clean, if he kept himself clean. But since I have taken you so far in, I might as well complete the job. As the story goes, after he has finished his dirtying business in his bathroom, two men step in with a long damp towel and passing the towel between his legs they stroke his bottom back and forth with it and he is as good as new again.

"Satta, Satta," rang and echoed the yard with his name as this human giant entered the gate. Visibly pleased by the spontaneous reception Satta surveyed the gathering with a heavily cushioned smile. He came to the large bed and eased himself into a reclining position against the huge pillow. Before his body could hit the pillow, one of his henchmen, standing behind, started squeezing and massaging him behind the neck and shoulders while another started squeezing his arm, more as a mark of veneration than as an exercise in physiotherapy.

Satta was the youngest of the Danewalla brothers. Danewallas had quite a reputation. They were embroiled in a long running feud with the equally notorious Shingaras of Jangewalla. But the battlefield generally was the city of Mumbai. It was all about controlling the private transport business in the city. Both the Danewallas and the Shingaras were giants in the field of moving people and goods in and around the metropolis. That is what was known about their entrepreneurial activities. If they had any other much more lucrative side-shows going for them, those were not commonly known and almost never mentioned, unless in whispers.

As Shaikh S'adi, the great Iranian philosopher poet put it so succinctly; seven beggars can sleep under one tattered quilt but no empire is large enough to accommodate two monarchs. The war is expected to last until one of the families is wiped out because quitting was out of the question, not only that it was a matter of honour but mainly because the vanquished group would be annihilated anyway. There were no half measures in this game. Even one surviving male member of the ousted family could destroy the entire victorious household, given the chance. Forgiving and forgetting was not even an optional subject in the curriculum of the education of the parties involved.

These are tough men and they do not die easily either. They say that in the days gone by, when these people had no access to firearms, murders were committed mostly with hatchets by decapitating their victims. And these were not the brand of hatchets that ever got buried. Having satisfied himself that the victim was really dead, the killer would want to ensure that he remained that way. He would traditionally place a brick or a piece of rock between the torso and its severed top. Otherwise he would be running the risk of the two components getting together and start walking.

Three of the six Danewalla brothers had already laid down their lives in this feud and had the status of martyrs in their community. Their family members and others of the clan would relate stories of their valour with the same zest that common people reserve for their gods and goddesses. As if reading the writing on the wall, Satta is often quoted as saying, “I am not going to die of malaria: You can bet your life on it.”

When a man from one of these families is shot dead in gangland style in the great metropolis faraway, shock waves are felt all over Punjab, which has its own share of responsive action. These murders have a sort of pattern; the two concerned clans shared the losses almost alternately. The mothers begged their sons and the wives implored their husbands to take the losses and stop the carnage. But no one knew how: Not taking your turn when it was your turn would be disastrous. It was sure to send the wrong signal and no one could afford to take that risk.

When Dhanna, the first of the Danewalla clan came to the city that was Bombay then he had not come to set up camp here. He had come with a cargo of food grain from Ludhiana in his truck, which against the wishes of his parents he had acquired by selling a huge chunk of their inherited agricultural land. He had argued with his parents, justifiably perhaps, that as it was inherited property, he had as much claim to it as they had. He had pushed his point home by insisting that since they had brought him into this world without his prior consent they were fully responsible for his wellbeing. This enterprising young man was perhaps not the ideal type that you would like to take home and proudly introduce to your parents as a dear friend.

Dhanna’s sole mate on the long journey to New Delhi and then onto Bombay, the financial hub of the nation, would be the boy whom he affectionately called Dipper. Dipper had his own reason for running away from home. His parents could not find a bride for him. Dipper was not choosey; all he wanted was a wife, just any female of the human species would do. But his parents failed to oblige and not because they did not try hard enough. If you were to prepare the most exhaustive list of eligible bachelors, whatever Dipper's real name, it would be missing from that list. Dipper was a nice boy but that was not sufficient to earn him eligibility as a bachelor. A lot, a whole lot more would be needed in his case. Dhanna had started calling him Dipper because he was cross-eyed and his left eye was smaller than its Alpha counterpart on the other side of his nose. The main occupation of Dipper was to keep Dhanna in good humour and to try to stay on his right side during these long, exhausting trips. You can say that he was Dhanna's Man Friday and he was good at his job.

Dhanna himself was quite good at shaking off boredom on the highway, shouting insults at drivers, who crossed him, for no obvious reason at all. Despite the limitations of his vocabulary on the subject, graphic descriptions of mothers' and sisters' anatomy featured repeatedly in his outbursts. He did all this without the least bit of malice, though. In fact he was quite good natured about it.

Back to the revelry of the wedding party; some members of the host family were in constant attendance on this elite group headed by Satta, who had retained all the pedigree traits of his ancestor, mentioned above. Drinks and snacks were now being served all around.

As Satta, the heaving heap of fat and flesh lay on the mega bed. Topialla, who had spent most of his youth in North America pursuing a literary profession, took a good look of disbelief and was reminded of the beached whale that he had once seen, the one that had died, having been crushed under its own weight.

The function was an all male affair, all, that is, except the entertaining quartet. You could, if you really wanted to put your imagination under pressure, call this spectacle a mellowed down version of a Western style stag party, mellowed down because there was no nude blonde about to jump out of a cake and again these festivities had their own unique tradition-imposed inhibitions.

The 'inhibitions' were conspicuous by their presence in the form of the elders who were scattered all over the place and who were content to keep the dying embers of their own residual passions buried under the ashes of time. They were not supposed to allow any leeway to their mind that might show signs of buckling when confronted by temptation.

When the singing women came close to these aging sons of the soil and made advances, regardless of whether these elders were musing on the lost opportunities that fate had offered them in their youth or on the opportunities that never came their way, they were consciously holding onto the stoic expressions on their faces, with a Herculean effort in most cases. Just as they were keeping a close watch on the youth, their conduct could be under scrutiny too.

Always on the lookout for someone holding out a currency note, the women were weaving their way through and around the clusters of tables and cots in the courtyard in every direction swaying their bodies with the beat of the music. Despite their skinny famished looks, they seemed to be full of vitality, dancing and singing:

"Glitter of the nose-pin..."

"I lost my nose-pin..."

There was a lot of hullabaloo with nothing musical about it but none was sober enough to care for music anyway. Emboldened by liquor, young men with their drunken eyes oozing lust were coming out of their seats and were making their offerings after twirling small bills over the heads of the singers.

But the women were after the big game. They do not get a chance to perform for such a prosperous gathering everyday.

One of the singers made a beeline for Topialla and putting her arm around his neck she pleaded, “Blessed be the topi; blessed be Topialla.”

Embarrassed by the sudden charge of this confounding attention, he dug into his wallet and handed her a fifty rupee bill.

There was visible amusement in the Satta camp. A henchman placed a hundred rupee bill between the lips of his boss.

The quartet was enthused by the spirit of competition that they had been able to whip up. Swaying wildly and making come-on gestures another one of them danced her way to the Big Boss and holding her heaving body over him she plucked the bill from his mouth with her lips, making sure that her lips touched his and then danced back centre stage. The henchmen celebrated with a victory shout.

As the sound of cheer subsided, one of Satta’s liegemen stood up in front of Satta’s divan and facing and staring at Topialla lifted his right hand, brought its back to his mouth and with his hand touching and leaving his lips intermittently made a loud vulgar sound known as the he-goat mating call even though there is absolutely no commonality between the *ba-ba-ba-ba* sound produced and the he-goat love call. The sound actually is made in an effort to mimic the mating call of a male camel as it blows through its blown out tongue making a throaty bubbly noise. This vulgarity is supposed to be the most provoking and insulting gesture in Punjabi culture.

Topialla knew the exact significance of the man’s taunt and he was visibly rankled but he was also not oblivious of his own vulnerability in his present situation. He knew he could not afford to stand up and face his adversaries. The odds were heavily stacked against him. He had no option but to decide that in the prevailing circumstances self-preservation should take precedence over any misplaced ideas of valour. Accordingly, making light of the affront, he stood up facing the monster, raised his right hand and smilingly made a mock saluting gesture, army style. Everyone, including the Satta gang, was amply amused.

All along, while this drama was being enacted, the dancing and singing went on uninterrupted. Pretending to be concerned about the 'reputation' of her hero, 'Topialla's girl' bounced back to him but before she could make any advances, he held out a hundred rupee bill keeping her at bay all the same. The fat man's team burst into laughter at Topialla's timid behaviour. The mountain of lard lying in bed shook with laughter like jelly and the gigantic bed shook with him. His swollen cheeks were threatening to eliminate the little space occupied by the slits of his eyes as he laughed.

Before long, Satta was holding a five hundred rupee note in his leering lips. Bankrolls were being snapped by his team-mates with a flourish to indicate hunger for competition.

It was Topialla's turn again. This time he was pretty sure of himself: he seemed to know what he was up to. As the girl approached him he showed no sign of reaching for the wallet, instead, as she came close, he moved closer and whispered something in her ear. The girl hesitated then retraced her steps walking backwards, struck an elaborate posture of obeisance to Topialla, turned and joined her group. As if she had accomplished her mission, she beamed with happiness.

Satta gang was a confused lot. What they had witnessed was not from the original script, so far as they were concerned. What irritated them the most was their ignorance of what exactly had happened. They knew that something underhand, perhaps a prelude to a larger conspiracy, had taken place. They were peeved no end because they had not the foggiest notion as to how to respond to this unknown factor.

In actual fact, Topialla had offered a hefty bribe to the dancers if only they would leave him alone. The offer was swallowed bait, hook, line and sinker with visible relish. But the Satta gang is never going to have the inside info on this deal. Now they started looking at Topialla with visible suspicion.

Satta did not like it one bit. He was bristling with anger. Topialla, it seemed, had in a high stakes game of cards, cheated a man whose forefinger was itching to squeeze the six-shooter. Satta lived by the law of the jungle, the only law that he recognized. The elephant bull that held his ground against any intruder was the unquestioned lord of the herd. The harem of impalas belonged to the stag that could beat the hell out of any other male in sight. Satta was not loved for his looks; he was held in awe because of the brute power that he wielded. Even within his own gang, his mates accepted gratefully what he doled out to them. The rest of the pride accepts humbly what the alpha lion after having feasted to his satisfaction, leaves of the kill for them, regardless of who made the kill. Satta was the alpha male of his pride, the undisputed king of his domain.

And here was a mouse-of-a-man-with-a-hat playing dirty tricks on him. The scores, Satta decided without mentioning it to anyone would have to be settled and settled before the night was out.

As the young men started getting soused up, the inhibitive barriers started crumbling down. They were becoming increasingly aggressive and started poking and grabbing as the women came within reach. In this restrictive society these are the rare chances for some of them when they could actually touch a young female body. It is interesting to note that there is a huge imbalance between the male and the female population in this part of India; approximately seven hundred females to every one thousand males. As a result, a sizeable number of these men are never going to get married.

O how they wished the elders were not there. The realm of possibilities boggled the mind. They were forgetting that but for the restraints imposed by the presence of the elders the women would not be there. But that realization did not trespass upon the fertile imagination of the youth.

One wonders whether the elders were dreaming of their prospects; speculating, what if the young ones were not there. Eager to be handled eager to be grabbed, the women offer fake resistance, accompanied by peals of laughter, cashing their favours on the spot. The elders try to give the impression that they were paying to get rid of them. The young are paying in the hope that they will be back for more. The shy ones leer sheepishly but pay up anyway. Business is booming. All are enjoying, most of them a bit uncomfortably.

At the edge of this action-packed drama and unnoticed by everyone, a baby is lying in the lap of a sickly looking nine year old girl. The girl is trained not to be a nuisance in any way but her eyes are glued to the goings on as her mom makes the rounds among the revellers. She winces every time a daredevil among the rustics tries to handle her mother. She feels as if the lusty hands were clawing her own skin where her breasts would be in their own time. Some day, in the not too distant future, those tentacles would be stretching out to explore her person. Chilled with horror she cringes as she watches.

A couple of young men from the bride's family came to announce that dinner was ready. Dinner was being served in a separate location adjacent to the bride's home. Rows of tables were arranged under a canopy. Waiters in starched white uniforms were serving food. Almost a quarter of the marriage party were unable to make it to dinner. They were too pickled, too full of food or both. Topialla was also not particularly hungry. But he decided to be present at dinner to make an appearance. As dinner concluded he did not feel like staying any longer. He had fulfilled his obligation of presenting himself at the wedding ceremony. Having settled his deal with the dancing girl, he slipped out unnoticed and went straight to his sporty Gypsy. He hit the road for the town where he intended to spend the night before driving home the next day.

After dinner the folding dining tables were removed from the enclosure and the chairs were rearranged leaving a sizeable arena in the middle. With silken handkerchiefs flowing from their wrists Satta's men jumped into the arena. They sang and danced with full vigour while Satta sat in an armchair smiling appreciably. One of the men would sing a folk song in a doleful voice and before he would finish his short song the men would hit the floor with lightening speed and go crazy dancing in circles.

On a hint from him one of Satta's men passed a hand bag on to him. Pulling out one thousand rupee bills from the bag Satta started doling them out to his men without much interruption in the dance performance. One by one each man bowed before him, placing his hands on Satta's feet and then touching his own forehead in obeisance. Satta then handed ten of those crisp bills to each one of his loyal men. Having received the money each one would then fold his hands in front of his boss and without turning would walk backward to join the dancing party. In appreciation of Satta's generosity the dancers, as if possessed by the furies, kicked up a frenzy that seemed to set the yard floor ablaze.

At the conclusion of the dancing and singing the fireworks started. Satta's party was now arranged in a ring and Satta, flanked by his men, was seated where the solitaire would be on an engagement ring. The whole village had gathered for this part of the celebrations. Women and children had also come out and had joined the fun. Specialists had been hired to light up the sky with rockets shooting up and bursting into hundreds of multicoloured stars. The bride's father had promised that the villagers would not be able to forget the event for the rest of their lives and that it would remain unmatched for as long as he lived. A battery of firecrackers exploded with deafening noise. Most of those present had plugged their ears to keep their eardrums from exploding. Screaming children were clinging to their mothers; scared boys and girls were running in every direction. It sounded like the scene of a battlefield.

Satta's head fell forward as he slumped in his chair. No one knew what had happened. His men panicked as they picked him up and tried to straighten him. The bullet had hit him above his right ear and had come out between his left eye and the left temple. Blood was flowing all over him. The fireworks had stopped and there was pandemonium all around as shouting, screaming men and women ran helter-skelter like headless chickens.

When the realization of what had happened dawned on the gathering everyone went numb and a long silence followed. In the hush they heard the distant sound of the racing Gypsy.

One of Satta's men looked around and shouted, "Where is Topialla?"

"Where is Topialla?" Another one echoed.

"Who is Topialla?" Yet another wanted to know.

"Topialla is gone."

"Topialla has fled." The uproar was spontaneous.

No one seemed to know who Topialla was, where he had come from or where he had gone. If someone did have any information on the subject, he decided to keep it to himself in the interest of personal safety. Silence was golden. This was no time to stand up and be counted.

"I had suspected foul play all the time. I never had any doubt in my mind; something had been going on between Topialla and the dancing girls?" An investigative mind was on a roll, bent upon redefining logic.

Leaving a couple of men with the dead body, the rest picked up their loaded arms and ran to their parked vehicles. They got into their vehicles and started racing in the direction of the fading sound of the Gypsy.

*****

Traffic Lights

When cold blooded senselessness
Takes over the collective human conscience
Transforming man to beast
Time is ripe for another
Big Bang.

I was in a jubilant mood when I and my gaiety decided to go for a hot bath, Indian style, sitting cross legged on the tiled floor of the bathroom with the hot water bucket in front and a large mug in hand to deliver the steaming energizer. Hot water trailing down the spine renders a soothing sensuous feeling.

I was yodelling a popular Kishore Kumar song and working up lather on my body at the same time when I got the feeling that I was adrift. The base of the body-beautiful was in motion. Sure enough my soapy bottom was sliding peacefully along the shining black granite tiles. For the buoyant mood though, the slide was a non-event. The frantic movements of the arms that they had been engaged in, with the intent of spreading the suds, went on uninterrupted to the beat of the yodel.

The grey matter on top was alert and operational at full throttle. Consequently, I was quick to discover that the bathroom floor had a slope; a slight slope but a slope all the same. It was enough of an excuse for the gravitational pull to navigate me successfully on towards the top of the drain in the corner. I stopped the dual exercise of yodelling and lathering and tried to find my bearings. As expected, I caught my bottom in the act of exchanging the neighbourhood gossip with the drain opening. Without opening my eyes, I knew instinctively that the hot water bucket was located somewhere to the southeast, a fair eight feet away.

I knew my physics well enough to remember the law of motion: A thing in motion remains in motion and a thing at rest remains at rest unless an outer force is applied ….. With soap on my face, eyes tight shut and the bathroom door bolted from inside it was pointless to think of launching an expedition in search of an outer force to arrest the waywardness of my impulsive posterior and bring me back to the neighbourhood of the hot water bucket. I opened my left eye a slit and discovered that the towel was hanging within easy reach. I picked it and its application to the face restored the sight. I struggled to gain the posture that bestowed the name homo-erectus to the human race. Finishing the bath, I was glad to emerge from the bathroom with body parts all intact and accounted for. I got dressed hastily and hopped into the car. My 'bigger' half was already in place in the front passenger seat, crouching and ready to pounce, demanding explanations for taking 'an eternity' to finish my toilet but with no intention of listening. Things were normal, on an uneven keel.

Has anyone been able to figure out the logic behind the installation of traffic lights? They are here, there and everywhere. One cannot drive a few metres without being confronted by the green, amber and red trio. They stand there and dare you. With the backing of the law of the land they browbeat you into submission. They curb your freedom of movement. They are an insult to the intelligence of the individual. They are a challenge to the ability of a person to determine when or where to bump or not to bump into another vehicle. They are 'roadblocks' in the path of your legitimate progress and an affront to the age-old established norm of the survival of the fittest. It is one thing to put dangerous, mentally disturbed persons in straight jackets, it is quite another to restrain sane people from driving around freely.

I am sure you did not know this. Traffic lights in most Indian cities are the result of a deep rooted conspiracy between the municipal authorities, beggars, and petty salespersons. As the lights turn red at an intersection, the beggars and petty vendors swarm you like you have hit a beehive. Before you know what is happening, you are being smothered in toilet paper rolls, incense, paper napkins and pirated movie DVDs. Newspaper boys howling sensational headlines and those who are seemingly busy cleaning the windshield of your vehicle, that is, if you are driving one, demand your attention. And the beggars simply refuse to be ignored.

Stupid red lights: Before they come to a stop at the intersection drivers scramble and jockey for positioning their vehicles to ensure a head-start when the lights would change to green. There is a shameless display of absolute disregard for traffic rules and human decency as drivers try to outsmart one another: A hair's breadth short of a demolition derby where cars wreck one another. You can call it a no-contact demolition derby. But the motor bikes and the scooters really stretch the limits. They worm their way wiggling and wriggling in and out through spaces around you that you did not know existed.

In 'other' societies, if a driver sticks his hand out of his vehicle, you can rest assured that he wants you to know that he is volunteering to surrender his right of way in your favour. But here in the prevalent law of the jungle when a driver puts his hand out of his vehicle it is invariably an ultimatum, a contemptuous angry gesture commanding you to desist from being in his line of thrust and warning you of the consequences because he is not going to reach for the brakes for the likes of you. He may, at best, press his horn angrily as his last split-second warning.

Again in societies mentioned above, if an oncoming vehicle flashes its headlights at you, the driver wants you to know that he has detected the presence of police on the highway so that you can reduce your speed to within the legal limits and avoid being ticketed. Contrarily, here when someone flashes his headlights at you he wants you out of his way and he wants you to comply fast. To make his point clearer he will tilt his steering wheel slightly in your direction. It is the ultimate in brinkmanship but you dare not attempt to call his bluff because you may not be there to realize that it wasn't after all a bluff, especially if the onslaught was dressed in a Sumo, Qualis or a Scorpio. And we haven't even introduced to you the native version of the Tasmanian devil of the Indian highways.

Take a truck driver (I do not mean literally take him somewhere, especially not to introduce him to your girl friend, that is, if you intend, at a future date, to be her worse half.). Fill this manipulator of heavy vehicles that you have taken, with a curried chicken. Bear with him while he washes his nourishment down with eight ounces of the 100 proof. Now unleash this doused specimen of manhood and despatch him on a nocturnal run on the GT Road, as our National Highway # 1 is historically known.

Stray dogs inhabit highways just as fish populate rivers and oceans. It is their natural habitat. When our heavy footed hero behind the wheel spots one of these God's creatures, there is lustre in his eye. He steps on the accelerator and - Bingo! What was once a scabies-stricken mongrel is now minced meat delicacy; delicacy for crows and not for the human palate. Did you know crows have no taste buds, nor any saliva? They just gulp their food down. What a waste and what a shame.

I can feel curiosity getting the better of you. You are itching to know: Why the crows, why not the vultures? A very intelligent query, if I may say so myself. Why not the vultures? Those of you with real foresight must have already guessed. Our truck driver's first cousin who was left behind to polish off his share of the curried proteins and, of course, the balance of the moonshine is driving what he adoringly calls his Buckey. He is known to allude to himself as Mirza. Now Buckey is no Tom, Dick or ___. What is meant is; Buckey is no factory line product Dodge, Ford or what-ya-may-call-it kind of a truck. It is a thoroughbred real live thing, the kind that leaves Maruti 800s fit for recycling and bumps Ambassadors off the pavement, except when they bear a crowning red light or a flag, even though the flag may be covered, indicating that the bigwig is not a part of the cargo.

By the way, the flagged cars are coming out again (after the restrictive period of the militancy days) like the tiny scarlet red rain bugs: *Veervohties* we used to call them, which come out after a rainfall in the countryside, except in Ludhiana, where the high pollution levels seem to have annihilated practically everything that crawls except the local *chamchas*, (no disrespect is intended to the useful items of cutlery originally known by this name). But the question still stares you in the eye: Why not the vultures?

Having failed to produce the required admission fee, I missed my chance when they offered an advance course in vultureology but surely you have studied these adorable birds that failed to collect their lift-off equipment at the supply depot. A vulture, unless of course its mother was crossed with an eagle, needs a fair length of runway for a takeoff, which you are going to insist, it has, the highway providing practically a limitless stretch of tarmac. And if I was quick thinking that day and had my presence of mind at that particular moment, I would retort: True, but not necessarily. The thoroughbred vulture i.e. the non-hybridized-non-crossed variety does not have the luxury of running along the highway to pick up speed, which is necessary for the takeoff, because it cannot outrun our Buckey, which is riding on its tail, especially when Mirza, throws the reigns on Buckey's neck, in a manner of speaking. So the vulture tries a takeoff across rather than along the highway but the odds are stacked heavily against a successful lift off; she never has a chance. The crow has a substantial edge for this feat.

For a pedigree crow it is easy as snatching candy from a child's hand, which it also does so masterfully that the child believes that the *koko* has taken it away. The crow is equipped for vertical landing and lift-off, which is vital for feasting on our national highways. Now, do not get me wrong. I am in no way suggesting that you need to be programmed for a vertical takeoff if you are eating on our national highways sitting inside your vehicle or in the *Pehalwan's Dhaba*, for that matter.

Now that is the primary reason I had a preference for the crow. And this should also explain the exclusion of the vulture from the guest list. And anyway, whoever heard of anyone having a vulture for a pet? I can say with certainty that if you were to choose between a crow and a vulture, the latter would not have an outside chance. If all this makes sense to you, congratulations and welcome to the club.

From which side are you supposed to pass a vehicle on the road? Depends on which side you can squeeze through. It makes sense too because the slowest moving vehicles normally occupy the supposed fastest lane. By the way, the lane concept has already been rejected by the South Asian public as too confusing and therefore impractical. Regardless of whether the lane markings are there or not the driver ahead of you will try his best not to let you pass and he does not need to pick up speed to accomplish that. He can do it by staying where you cannot pass him on the right or the left even if he has to swerve this way or that to keep you behind.

If a vehicle hits you from behind, it is always your fault because you broke the rules by slowing down, by applying the brakes in an effort to save a careless pedestrian or by simply being in the path of a speeding vehicle. You are supposed to keep your vehicle out of other people's way and other people come from all directions in all modes of Indian transport.

If you do get into a fender-bender bump with another vehicle, watch how the driver of the other vehicle views the situation. If he seems apologetic about his role in the accident, consider it to be your lucky day. But normally it does not happen that way here. If, as is quite probable, the driver of the other party happens to come out of his vehicle and appears to be approaching you equipped with a tyre lever, a wrench or a hammer, you can be sure that the driver in question is not coming to tighten the nuts on your car wheels or to fix the dent in your car. The fact is that he believes, rightly or wrongly could be a debatable issue, that the dent in your car is way off its mark and that it should have been located at some suitable site on your head instead and further that he intends to rectify the wrong on the spot. Never try to apply logic in a situation like this. Because no matter how weighty your reasoning might be, a tyre lever and its associates are in a weight class of their own. Your best option would be to quickly confess that the accident was the result of your gross negligence.

If the accident is of a more serious nature and you end up with a couple of broken legs dangling under you, consider this to be your lucky day because you are safe from the evil temper of your adversary. The problem in a situation like this is that the police will arrive long before an available ambulance and its driver can locate each other, considering that there is an ambulance somewhere in the vicinity and also that the driver has reported on duty instead of going off to attend his third cousin's wedding. Some ambulances even have to carry patients to hospitals. Their main job though is to transport high officials' families to shopping malls and restaurants. It is a well known fact that the cops can smell blood a lot faster than the paramedics can. The police also have the exclusive right to bodies, dead or alive. Top among the priorities of the police is to get 'your' statement of facts relating to the unfortunate (for you) accident. But they are always very helpful about it. They would write it down for you themselves without much input from you. All you have to do is sign on the dotted line.

Now it is your role to pursue one of the three options:

Firstly, you may want to call your influential uncle in the Ministry of Home Affairs and let him get you out of the soup. Secondly, you may opt to fight your case in a court of law in a strange city with the knowledge that the case may drag on for years. Needless to point out that during these years you will have to suspend all of your other activities, making a livelihood among them. You will be busy trying to catch up your lawyer who has in all probability received more money from your adversary in the case, behind your back, than you intend to pay him. The third option, which is your best bet if you do not have an influential uncle or if he is in not in his 'oblige' mode, is to come to terms with the police. Being the authors of 'your' 'confessional' statement, they know that the stakes are high and that the odds are stacked against you. You are a novice at this game while they are seasoned players. Emotionally also they are far better placed than you are: While you are thinking of your extended stay in the hospital with your broken legs, they are thinking about a night on the town with mountains of roast chicken and a steady flow of whisky to ease it down with. They squeeze you hard and you cough up obligingly. Not until they are finished with you to their satisfaction, will the stretcher come out of the ambulance. Such is the unscripted but well respected law of the land.

At railway crossings when the gates are closed to allow a train to pass, vehicles are supposed to occupy the entire width of the road on both sides of the gates; such is the prevalent tradition. When the gates open, the floodgates open. Try to remember a historical movie: It is the middle ages and in a battle for supremacy the mighty armies clash head on across the spread of the battlefield. Blaring horns effectively substitute the war trumpets while at the same time they caution those who might have gone to sleep on the wheel that the gates are now open and that it is time to wake up and get going. For the next few minutes at least, all traces of humane feelings, of compassion or even of decent social conduct are put to rest Utter shamelessness rules the roost You are surrounded on all sides by enemies whose sole aim in life is to crush you out of existence. They bear upon you from all sides and you are to muscle your way out of this tightening noose and surge ahead shouldering them out of your path. Your vehicle is not simply your means of transport, in moments of need such as this it is an effective weapon and your shield against personal injury. Other people in the fray have no feelings at all and if they have, they are none of your concerns. The idea is to forge ahead and stay ahead at all cost. Whether you have time at your disposal to spare is irrelevant to the situation. When you are on the open highway and there is no competition, you can slow down and take it easy to dispel your tension but here in this congestion you cannot be put down and held back. It is simply not acceptable.

If you are used to driving on black ice in Canadian winters you will have no problem driving in Indian summers because melted tar on the hot pavement behaves exactly like frozen ice which, a keen observer in Canada will discover, it may be useful to mention in passing, is the only kind of ice found in that country.

Bear in mind, in this country, i.e. India, the 'book' tells you to drive on the left side. But the 'book' doesn't drive and people don't drive by the 'book'. They have not heard of it. At an intersection when the lights are red the traffic comes to a standstill, that is, if there is visible police presence in the immediate neighbourhood. Just remember that even though we are supposed to drive on the left side of the road the vehicles that are to turn right are all jammed in the left lanes. It is advantageous for them to be there rather than being behind the vehicles in the right lane. When the lights are about-to-turn-green, the right-turning vehicles cut across the vehicles to their right like lightening. If you are a sprinter in a competitive sense, you don't wait for the 'o' in 'go' before you cross the starting line. You leap forward to catch the 'g' somewhere between the starter's mouth and your ear and you are damned if you let the 'o' catch you at the starting line.

In the stormy sea of pressing vehicles, heat and the noise of blaring horns, I saw the red lights coming on and was thus trying to position my car in anticipation of the great push when the lights would turn green.

The leper's festering stump of a hand goes right into the wife's face through the open passenger side window before the car came to a stop.

"I am hungry", said the beggar trying to accommodate as much misery on her face as its inchage would permit. (Now be reasonable; if there are words like acreage, yardage and footage, what is so ghastly wrong about inchage? Anyway whose story is it?)

"I thought you might have been, honey. I have already booked a table for two at Lord's this evening in anticipation of your desire for nourishment. Would you care to join me? Don't bother to dress up, come as you are." I said to the beggar. Obviously the lady was not amused. She twitched her nose at me and I accepted it as a subtle hint that she had some other more pressing engagement and that she would not be able to grace the proposed rendezvous with her presence.

And I was in no mood to enter into a fruitless argument on behalf of the wife (of course, I mean my wife) but if I wanted to I had a very strong case against the logic as applied by the beggar.

I would start somewhat on these lines:

"In your case there seems to be nothing seriously objectionable in being hungry. But for the hunger, lady, you wouldn't have this 'job'. And without this job, you would starve anyway. Hunger suits your style of life; lends honesty of purpose to your chosen profession,"

I would have tried to reason it out if the beggar and I were dealing one-on-one and on an equal footing: if we were on a level playing field, so to say. But her affliction gave her an unquestionable edge. Realizing my handicap, better sense prevailed and I let the wife (Yes! the same) take care of her problem. The leper's stump was nowhere near MY face.

The blessed driver behind me jammed his hand on the horn button and let it rest there. This was his subtle way of counselling me to take wing and fly over the traffic and out of his way.

All 'conventional' sources having dried up and work for a living never having been tapped as an option, where the dough is to come from, I do not have the foggiest. But I have firm faith in providence. The Lord provides sustenance to the micro organisms that he creates in the bosom of the stones. He feeds the parasite and the host of the parasite. He is the creator and in the fitness of things Hc should be the sustainer too. He cannot be allowed to just create and then let go. Persistently and determinedly I have refused to accept any responsibility for creating myself. Creation is not my volition. I am not in competition with the Lord. I am not in this world subject to my own sweet will. I did not jump into this hellhole to be even a spectator, much less to be a performer. Why should I be penalized for being in existence? Why should I be responsible for supporting myself? I did not consciously or even unconsciously opt for being delivered into this dog-eat-dog world.

If, being in my senses and through my own volition, I can be prevailed upon to bring any offspring into this vale of tears, logic demands that they are at least partially my responsibility and that I must take care of them. But I had no hand in placing myself on the surface of a miserable stretch of this already overpopulated madhouse. I place the blame where it belongs. As such I like to think of myself as a respectable conscientious parasite of society.

To make a conservative estimate, the sum of five million rupees, to round off the figure, is rather crucial: The wife's damned brother has outgrown the condominium that I had bought for him. Threatens, he is coming 'home' unless I provide him accommodation in step with the need of times and to suit his station in today's society. The wife jumps into the fray hysterically on such occasions, cursing me for the high social status that I had thrust on her unsuspecting brother, by seducing and hitching with his baby sister.

The plot is thickening rather fast. But trust me as I say to you: The pieces of the puzzle will fall in place in due course and the narration will make perfect nonsense.

"Are you blind? Can't you see?"

That now is the wife on the warpath launching a two pronged offensive, taunting the beggar for her rash behaviour and in the same breath accusing me of inaction. A flawless strategy, if I may say so myself. The wife's single rapid burst of fire aimed at the border infiltration as well as the home front was a masterful stroke of a rare martial genius. Under the massive, merciless impact, the stump recoiled. After the initial setback and the sudden retreat which was more a knee-jerk reflexive action than a considered strategic move, the stump bounced back.

With her defences crumbling down and sensing imminent peril, the wife decided to release some white doves. She picked an olive branch and waving it frantically, she blurted out a conciliatory note:

"Why don't you work for a living?"

In times of dire need, the missus has a few pillars of strength to lean on; most dependable among whom is her big (really big) brother, who is irrelevant to the present sit. The most conspicuous among those pillars though, is logic, by its very absence. Obviously, she did not give any credit to the stump that occupied the site where a working hand would have been located under normal circs.

"For ever and evermore, may you be together as a couple," prayed the beggar.

The miserable wretch comes begging, and spells curses too.

"Are you just going to sit there and watch?" The wife questions me.

I have the answer on my lips; it has been there, seemingly, forever. It has been mentally rehearsed and re-rehearsed a million times. But it never escaped my lips. But I have no qualms about sharing it with you, the reader, as a sort of an 'aside':

"Of course I would not want to sit here and do nothing. Among some of my favourite things, I would love to waltz on the sacred ground that covered you and held you and your creeping, crawling companions in its dark and dingy bosom."

But for her blasted brother, that would have been my response. There are more where that one came from, each one a masterpiece in its own unique way. But the lout has no sense of humour: Can't take a joke for what it is worth.

"Roll up the window darling." I suggested.

"With that thing in?" That was her.

In sheer desperation, I threw up both my hands.

For beggars, brothers in law, and may be their baby sisters, if only mass burials could be legalized, this world with its beauty and splendour would be a heavenly place.

Without the hungry rotting around, there won't be hunger any more. And without the brother-in-law and his baby sister, by God, I won’t need the millions either; well, not so desperately.

The lights changed to green. A thousand horns screamed clarion calls in unison to ensure that all have seen the changing lights.

The traffic moves again and we are carried with the flow. Believe you me, the juicy words that the beggar shot at us as we moved on without giving her any money and parted company with her are not even a part of your passive vocabulary nor that of any dictionary: Supremely educative.

*****

Of Fishes and Crocodiles

Finger nails crack and principles bleed as
Man tampers with a solid state destiny
That was delivered sealed and secured:
The writ left no blanks to be filled in by man.

Future on the mend?
It blasts past; the present is obliterated,
Trashed into the oblivion of the past before impaction.

On the conveyor belt of destiny
Man is presented to the robotized hands of fate
That deal programmed events and happenings;
Pain and anguish punctuated by an occasional laughter.

And man thinks he is alive and
That he even has a will.

I had met Gowardhan the first time at my young orchard. We were busy digging holes for planting apple saplings in an, as yet, unplanted section of the orchard. Gowardhan, I knew, was not a part of the work force. Being middle aged and weak he was unemployable for the kind of back breaking work that was in progress. The loamy clay earth that was being dug would have been soft and pliable during the monsoon season but in November, the planting season, it was rock hard. The earth was stony and the huge boulders that sometimes had to be grappled with and extricated needed muscles of steel. In Gowardhan's case, there was hardly anything between his skin and bones. He was a lean thin man of medium height. If the breadth of his boney shoulders was any indication he must have had a powerful physique not many years earlier. The strong young men comprising the working group at my orchard were all petty peasant farmers who worked as unskilled manual laborers anywhere they could find employment. This way they earned money to supplement the meager income from their agricultural land. Most work that they found was seasonal and temporary.

Kathu, my supervisor of operations, had informed me that Gowardhan had particularly come to see me. With the end of the tape measure held by Kathu I was busy marking the exact spots where the holes were to be dug. There must be exactly twenty five feet between the plants on all sides and the plants must be alternated between one row and the next to make diagonal straight rows of plants in both directions throughout the entire area of the orchard. We were working on the mountain slope therefore it took a lot of calculation and planning. I had my hands full. Gowardhan also seemed to be in no hurry. It was during the lunch break that I had called him into the small makeshift room to find out what he wanted. I invited Gowardhan to share our lunch with us while he told me that he had a small piece of land in the neighboring village and that he wanted to sell it to me. (Kathu had later informed me that he had no family and that it was the last piece of Gowardhan's petty landholding. A little bit at a time, grudgingly, it would seem, he had disposed it all off.) I informed him that the plot of land that he was offering for sale was so small and so far from my land that it would be useless for me. Dejection on Gowardhan's face was writ large as he listened to me.

"But why is it so important for you to sell this land?" I had enquired. Gowardhan had glanced at my supervisor awkwardly. Kathu spoke for him, "Sir, he needs the money badly." And to illustrate Kathu's remark, Gowardhan made a motion with his hand as if he were putting a morsel of food into his mouth. Gowardhan was hungry and he was well past his prime and in failing health. Being unskilled and weak he had no place in the job market where able bodied young men found it hard to get employment.

I did not have the heart to turn down his request while at the same time I also did not want to deprive him of the only worldly possession that he had. I paid him the petty amount quoted by him as price of his property but I had no intention of transferring the land to my name. He hesitated in accepting the money.

"Sir, the payment could wait until the land transfer deed was completed," he said apologetically.

"As you can see Gowardhan, I am awfully busy at the moment. But there is no hurry. I shall call you to the Patwari's office when I have some free time and then we can go through the formality of the transfer deed." I offered my excuse.

He looked sheepishly at Kathu and me alternately as he bade good bye and walked out of the door.

It was a few months later that I met him the second time when I saw him digging and turning the soil under the apple trees in Seth Dhani Ram's orchard which was adjacent to the Seth's home and his provision store. It was early evening. Gowardhan gave me a weak smile as he greeted me. In fact I was going to the Seth's provision store to pay some bills for the groceries that I had been ordering. The Seth was very friendly. He always offered me a chair even though he preferred to sit cross-legged on a mat. Every time I paid him a visit, he would insist on me accepting a cup of tea which was prepared in his home that was in the same building.

It was quite late at night when after having my dinner at the local eatery I was returning to my little room at the orchard that I saw Gowardhan still working in the orchard. This was no time for anyone to be working in an orchard. It was a chilly night and the thought of someone working so late was disturbing to say the least.

"Isn't it a bit too late to be working out?" I almost shouted at him.

Then he explained it to me. He would stop working only when he was called to get his routine limited supply of meals comprising boiled rice with a touch of lentil. Only when the Seth family was ready to go to bed would he get his food. The Seth would want to extend his working hours to the possible limit.

Gowardhan was paid no wages other than the two scanty meals per day. He told me his sad story. After running through the money that I had given him he had no option but to borrow for his groceries from the Seth. He knew and the Seth knew that he had no means of paying the loan back. He now was what is known as a bonded laborer. I asked him how much he owed the Seth. "Only the Seth would know that Sir," was his naïve answer.

The next day I went and met Gowardhan a little early. I asked him to accompany me to the Seth's store. I instructed him to ask the Seth about his loan in my presence. At first he refused to accompany me admitting that he was scared of antagonizing the Seth. But on my insistence he grudgingly started following me.

When we reached the store the Seth wanted to know what Gowardhan was doing there. Why was he not at his work? Gowardhan had nothing to say. He did not even look at the Seth once. Finally I informed the Seth that Gowardhan would like to know how much he owed him. Gowardhan was sitting on his feet and was staring blankly at them. The Seth said that he would know the amount when he had the money to pay back. I told the Seth that he had the money. The Seth was incredulous.

"Has he robbed a bank?" He wanted to know.

"I am lending him the money." I explained.

The Seth looked at me accusingly as if I had betrayed his friendship.

"Sir, you will never see your money again." He warned me.

"I am hiring him to work at my orchard." I said simply.

"He owes me one hundred twenty rupees," said the Seth, after consulting his records.

I paid the money and took Gowardhan to the local eating place. It was a rare joy to watch him filling himself awkwardly. With a sense of elation I took him to his home and instructed him to report for work at my orchard the next morning. I told him that he would be handing tools to the laborers and serving water to whomsoever wanted it and that he would get the same wages as the other workers were paid. He felt very happy and relieved. I thought he would never stop thanking me.

***

I had a vague idea of what I was getting into. But Arvinder Singh Thakur was such an affectionate student that I did not have the heart to say no when he invited me to accompany him to his family's homestead in the Outer Siraj valley of the Kulu district across the River Satluj from Virgarh. I had another reason for accepting the invitation: The school was closed for the short spring break. I had my own young orchard in the vicinity of Arvind's home where I intended to get some work done.

At that time I was posted as an English and Science teacher at the Government High School at Virgarh in the heart of the famous apple growing heavenly Himalayan slopes of Kotgarh. Arvinder Singh was the son of an apple grower who owned a medium sized orchard that was too young at that time to bear any sizable crop. My apprehension about the proposed visit was based on the fact that Virgarh High had no class without some of Arvinder's siblings on its roll. Ours was a coeducational boarding school and Arvinder and his six siblings were resident students. And most of them spent their weekends at home. Considering that houses on these beautiful hillsides were quite unimposing to put it mildly, (We are talking about the early sixties.) overcrowding was going to pose a serious problem. Shikha, Arvinder's beautiful sister who was also in Grade X with him accompanied us on the trek. The rest of the clan, I guessed, must have left earlier. From Virgarh it was a steep descent of four thousand and five hundred feet down to the River Satluj. We crossed the River at Luhri in a primitive squeaky wooden contraption, meant to substitute a trolley, by pulling a rope tied to an improvised fixture across the river. It was a horrifying experience even though the locals never gave it a second thought. We traveled about five kilometers down along the bank of the Satluj. From hereon, leaving the river behind, we ascended along the steep bank of a tributary of the Satluj climbing about a thousand feet in the next thirteen kilometers. Late in the evening we reached Ani at the bottom of a narrow valley with rising mountain slopes on both sides of the stream that we had followed. The lush green slopes to the north of the stream with pine at the lower elevation and cedar and fir forests at the higher altitude were pock marked with tiny houses surrounded by their small terraced fields and orchards. Close to the top of this mountain was one of my two young apple orchards. The other was located a couple of hundred feet lower and about 1km from the hub village of Chowai that boasted of a provision shop, a post office, a Forest Range Office and a country version of a restaurant. Apart from this Chowai was the headquarters of the Patwari, the lowest ranked official of the government land revenue department.

Along with my two escorts, I had left Virgarh in the mid afternoon and it was getting quite dark so against the insistence of my companions to continue our journey to reach their home that night, I decided that we should spend the night in the Public Works Department (PWD) Rest House at Ani. We checked into two rooms and ate whatever was available before retiring.

The next day we started around midmorning after a heavy greasy brunch of stuffed *prathas* with yoghurt and butter, finishing our meal with steaming hot sweet tea that left a sticky sugary taste on the lips. We retraced our steps going down along the stream for a couple of kilometers before crossing it. From here to Broti, it was a steep climb around a cliff. Despite being in my youthful mid-thirties, I was exhausted and out of breath as I stepped onto the flat lush green plain overlooking the beautiful valley around. The spot offered a fantastic view in every direction. The State of Himachal Pradesh is aptly known as the *Devbhoomi* 'The Land of the Gods' for two reasons; first, practically each little habitation, each little hamlet has its own god; and second, the natural beauty of the landscape and the simplicity and honesty of its people make it a fit abode for gods; not to mention the angelic beauty of its women.

When we reached the Thakur habitation my eyes rested on something that stuck out like a sore thumb in these otherwise heavenly surroundings; something that did not relate to the pastoral scene in general. It was almost noontime and a young man was sitting cross-legged on a cot inside a mosquito net at the edge of the young orchard and at a respectable distance from the homestead. The mosquito net was meant to keep the flies out. He had a glass in his hand; a bottle and a water jug were lying handy on a small stool by the side of his cot. You might think it was a bit too early in the day for such an indulgence but he was drinking. The way that he was sitting alone and drinking at this hour suggested that he was not a member of the family and also that he was being entertained.

On seeing me with my young companions he decided that I was not a member of their family either. With a drunken smile on his face he addressed me, "Brother, if you want real service, get in." and as if to put his signature on the invitation, he lifted the side of the mosquito net enough so that I could squeeze in. I sat inside the net with my legs hanging down the side of the bed. "Please be comfortable. Think of it as your own home. No need to observe any formalities." He added with a chuckle. Seeing me joining the young man my students left me and ran into the house.

Once partially inside the net, I realized that I was in a very awkward position. I was so well loved and respected by my students and their parents. This here was a man devoid of any shred of scruple whose name I did not know and who was obviously freeloading on my hosts for reasons best known to those concerned. What in the name of whatever is sacred to me was I doing being chummy with him.

I extricated myself from the confinement of the net and the man's sphere of influence with as much propriety as was possible under the circumstances and making myself scarce to him I hurried toward the family home with a parting "Excuse me, but I must pay my respects to the Thakurs first." thrown in the general direction of the man in the net.

My students must have been feeding their parents some real good stuff about me because Mr. Thakur and his wife were genuinely happy to see me.

Mr. Thakur was quite apologetic about the presence of the stranger on his property. The young man, Darshan Kumar, I was informed, was a Forest Range Officer who had supervised the construction of some retaining walls on the Thakur property. The forest department was erecting retaining walls in privately owned orchards and farms as a part of the prevention of soil erosion program. The boozy entertainment apparently was a 'thank you' gift to the supervising officer.

Arvinder informed me a little later that Darshan Kumar had fallen asleep and was snoring his head off. Meanwhile Mr. Thakur, accompanied by his children, took me for a stroll around their orchard. The kids were having a great time sniggering and aping snoring sounds as they danced around us joyously. Apart from informing me about the development plans for his orchard, Mr. Thakur gave me a few useful tips on raising my young orchard.

Late in the evening, Darshan Kumar woke up quite sobered and apologetic. He wanted to leave for his headquarters in Chowai right away but Mr. Thakur would have none of it. I informed

Darshan Kumar that I was also going to Chowai the next morning and that I would be happy to accompany him.

During the trek to Chowai in the company of Darshan Kumar I realized that contrary to my initial impression, he was quite a likeable young man. On reaching Chowai, he insisted that I be his guest for the day and that he would love to accompany me to my orchard the next morning. Before I could respond to his invitation, he dispatched one of his rangers to my orchard to fetch my supervisor from there to come and receive my instructions on the work to be undertaken in the mean time.

Darshan came with me to the orchard the next day and informed me that my orchard would be suitable for building retaining walls and a drainage system which would not cost me a penny. The entire project would be an undertaking of the Forest Department. Before bidding him Goodbye and leaving for my school, I made an appointment with him for that project for my next vacation.

***

Months passed before I could visit my orchard again. But I kept my appointment with Darshan Kumar for the construction of the retaining walls and the drainage system.

As I was passing by Seth Dhani Ram's orchard on the first evening after my arrival in Chowai, I was once more greeted by the familiar sight: Gowardhan was at work turning the soil under one of the apple trees. On seeing me he greeted me with a sad smile. "Sir, I am really sorry to have put you through so much unnecessary inconvenience but I can't fight destiny. I have to live in this river; I can't afford to antagonize the crocodile. You have been very kind Sir. God will reward you for that." Having resigned himself to his fate, he seemed to be at peace with the world.

As I walked on, I felt like a defeated warrior. The Seth saw me from a distance and greeted me heartily. I stepped into his store and took my usual seat in the chair. Without even asking me he shouted to the store attendant, “Hey Boy, Get Sir a steaming hot cup of tea.”

“Sir, you need not worry your head off on account of Gowardhan. He is OK the way he is. No one can do much about people like him.” The triumphant Seth was gloating as he smiled shamelessly.

I had no desire to talk about Gowardhan. I had no fight left in me and I wanted to put the whole episode behind me. But the Seth seemed to relish the subject.

“Sir, a worm of the gutter belongs to the gutter. Let it be.” He expanded on his philosophy.

Without realizing the enormity of the impact of his words, he had touched a raw nerve. The cup of tea remained untouched.

“How much does he owe you this time?” I demanded firmly.

*****

Bala

Not Mona Lisa
Nor the most acclaimed masterpiece
Of a Michelangelo
Not even the once-in-a-generation
Work of a literary stalwart
Holds the charm of the unforgettable
Folk tales my grandma told.

"Tell us a story," she said, as usual.

As usual, she laughed and laughed as she spoke. You're bound to think she was a child. Perhaps in her own special way she was.

Normally human beings grow up physically, intellectually and emotionally in a balanced manner. When some grown up person behaves like a child, you are apt to say, "Hey, grow up." Obviously you are not happy because that person is not acting their age. A lot better is expected of that person. But sometimes nature freaks out.

At forty, Bala was a happily married woman. She had a doting husband and three beautiful healthy children. Bala had matured and developed physically and intellectually and was in perfect health. Emotionally though she was still a child four years of age.

She started calling me uncle when we first met but before we said goodbye to each other she gave me a sudden promotion, addressing me as Daddy.
"Uncle, please tell us a story, then I have to go." She pleaded.

She sat cross-legged on the carpet, almost touching my foot as I sat in a chair. She had granted herself a mini break from the voluntary work in the community kitchen that catered to the twelve hundred odd volunteer *sevadars*.

Master was visiting the metropolis.

The *sevadars* performed all kinds of duties at the venue of the Master's discourses where thousands were in attendance. The sevadars were responsible for directing the traffic and conducting the audience to their seats apart from making general security arrangements.

A small gathering of disciples, we were lodged in the home of a generous couple. We were scattered in the living room in all kinds of comfortable postures in the chairs and on the carpet.

Expectancy was in the air. Having been touched by their Master in their own unique way, every disciple has stories to tell; I have some.

“Uncle, I have to go soon, will you please tell us a little story?”

She was unsure and a bit apprehensive because her break was short and coming to an end.

"Once upon a time, long ago," I began, "There was a very old man."

Tiny fog cushions were already beginning to press against her eyes.

The interjection is regretted, but as far as I can remember the only time she ever stopped laughing was to take some time off to shed a tear; sometimes not even then: She was so emotional you might think she was mad as a hatter. But aren't we all when we are in love? Was Jesus Talking about her when he said that we have to be like children in order to enter the kingdom of heaven?

Yes she was in love. So, I hear was Meera, the Rajput princess. But Bala, I know was in love. If symptoms point to the latent affliction, she was madly in love with her Master.

She wrote her own love songs, like Meera. Like Meera she sang her lilting lyrics, punctuating her music with peels of laughter, laughter of the contagious category. Bala's love was love fulfilled, love that holds hearts in the spell of its bounty.

During the shortest week of my present life, as I had known this bundle of vitality, totally oblivious of what she was up to, she tugged and pulled at my heartstrings no end. This was the fullest blown infancy that I had ever met; a symbolic child of universal innocence, showing no signs of any erosion of her nursery school charm. She was bathed in an aura of perpetual euphoria and blessed by her Master, she was divinely intoxicated.

She looked at me wide eyed with expectation.

"Yes," she urged me on.

Lord! Come Sunday it will be 'good bye'. I will be on my way to a distant home, stretching out taut my heart strings. Like nobody ever loved before, I loved her like she was the only daughter that I never had.

"The old man was the disciple of a great saint," I continued in the manner of a doting father singing a lullaby to his baby daughter in her little cradle.

"Having served well at his Master's Holy Feet, the old man had attained salvation during his lifetime and came to the end of the trail as we all will."
A couple of pearls had formed in Bala's sad eyes, her humble offering at her Master's Holy Feet.

"So one night he gathered his family around him and told them that his time had come; his Master was taking him back to the Primal Home."

The streams of tears were unbroken and flowing. Unashamedly, Bala was miserable.

“The old man explained the purpose of the meeting:

‘By the ultimate grace of my Master, I am going straight to *Sach Khand*, the Realm of Truth. So it is really an occasion to rejoice and not a time to mourn,’ said he.

“He went to great lengths in explaining to his wife, but especially to his loving daughter.

‘I plead with you, my child,’ he said, ‘when I am dead I will only have dropped off my old worn out body, releasing the soul in her pristine glory. It is all in the fitness of things because I am going beyond the field of mind and matter. So please do not mourn my death. Please don't cry, I beg of you because any action that could distract my attention could possibly place hurdles in my passage Home.’ ”

Catching at last the drift of the story, Bala became self conscious. She wiped her tears and sat up straight.

"During the night the old man dropped his mortal coil. The family was miserable and yet they were showing a lot of constraint. An unseen tear may be; an unheard sob, perhaps, but on the whole, the family exhibited a lot of fortitude and remained true to the last wish of the departed man.

“Things went on as smoothly as they could, given the circumstances. Bearing the loss was tough enough, as it was, tougher yet was the total ban on crying.

“The customary bathing of the mortal remains proceeded without any serious calamity except that the old man was dead and that was a calamity of sorts, that is, if you insist on looking at it from that angle.

“At the risk of repeating myself, I must say that things went quite well until, that is, it was time to wrap the body in the customary white sheet.

“The old man’s daughter took one good look at the wrapped up figure, lifted her face skyward and as if inspired by the full moon, she gave vent to the loudest howl ever heard on this side of the Tundra.

“As if all they needed was a cue, the household joined in a chorus and with gusto."

Bala was tense but she refrained from adding her voice to the wailing.

"Then as suddenly as she had started, the daughter stopped: She stopped crying and stood, petrified, struck dumb, as if she had seen a ghost, which in a way she thought she had. What she had actually seen was scarier than a run-of-the-mill ghost.

“She was staring at the body. She could swear she saw the right foot move. The whole clan witnessed, each in their own turn, what she had seen. The right leg moved and then slowly but surely the left leg too showed signs of life."

Bala was pressing her fingers against her wide open mouth.

"The family was running helter-skelter, each for himself but mostly for herself. The daughter turned for another look and she screamed her lungs out, this time not because her father was dead but because he was not dead enough.

“Slowly but surely the old man came back to life. He took off what was supposedly his last attire and donned the white sheet as a loincloth. Without the formality of a preamble or an introductory note the old man lunged and grabbed his walking stick that was standing dutifully in the corner at the exact spot where he had left it before calling it quits, as if in its own dumb way the stick had some premonition of his return visit. The old man had parted company with his stick because he did not think he would have much use of this extra baggage where he was going. Armed and exhibiting feline agility he leapt after his daughter."

Bala exploded with a burst of laughter. Holding onto her sides she swayed like a sapling surprised by an out of season hurricane.

"He let her have a few of the juiciest as she repeated her promise never to cry if he decided to die again.

“But that was not the problem on top of the old man's priority list because, as he explained, he had been condemned to live another week in this world of mind and matter before he could accompany his master to Sachkhand.

“ ‘Can't you Dad, if you really tried hard, of course at your convenience, die at an earlier date?’ ” The girl was really sorry for the inconvenience she had caused her beloved father.

Bala was now rolling on the carpet. The pain of laughter was too much to bear.

“But the poor old man was made to live off his attachments through a troubled week for all concerned.”

Laughing and staggering Bala danced out of the room.

*****

Scarecrow

In our dreary nook of the creation
Where pain and misery abound
A little nonsense
Makes more sense
Than volumes of sane literature
Written in blood and
Bound in hard covers.

Gian Singh's wife Sushminder claimed, with or without justification that royal blood ran through her veins: Not simply because she had peaches and cream complexion but because she could trace her lineage back to the royal family of an erstwhile princely state of Punjab. She had an iron will and an indomitable spirit. She was dignified and had a couple of inches over her husband in height. But the striking feature of her character was that she was extremely jealous by nature and was obsessively possessive of her husband. Gian Singh had never given her any reason for suspicion but that did not stop her from believing that the entire female population of the human species had been created to tempt and seduce her husband. And she never lost an opportunity to accuse him of looking at some lady sweetly, as she would put it; or some woman eyeing him shamelessly. In her presence he had to be very careful of his conduct where women were present, especially if they were of the feminine persuasion.

In sharp contrast to his wife, Gian was quite deficient in the looks department. Not many people remembered how he looked before his beard started encroaching on most of the available surface on his face except his nose, which sported a large mole on its tip decorated with its own circumjacent ring of hairy growth. He was a lawyer by profession and not very good at that either.

Once when they were a newly married young couple, Gian Singh and Sushminder were at a party hosted by the local Bar Association. Drinks were flowing freely and everyone was getting ready to have a good time when a young lady lawyer who was one of those who had organized the party came up to Gian Singh and tried to strike a conversation by asking him if he was enjoying himself. He went immediately on the defensive by introducing her to his wife. The lady claimed that she was 'pleased to meet' Sushminder. She started talking in general terms addressing both but looking mainly at Gian Singh's upturned face. Gian Singh was so enchanted by this sudden attention from unexpected quarters that he failed to notice that his wife's face had already changed a few colors. Sushminder pulled her husband away by the arm a little unceremoniously and insisted on going home immediately. Gian Singh saw no reason to leave the party but obliged her anyway.

Once at home, he demanded an explanation. Why did they have to leave the party, he wanted to know.

"What do you think she was doing pushing her big breasts into your face?" She was red in the face.

"She is a tall lady but what has that got to do with me?"

"Don't I know what was going on there? Your lady was ready to start suckling you in full public view if we had stayed there any longer. And don't act as if you don't know what she was up to. And you did not mind it at all. You seemed to be enjoying yourself." She said accusingly.

Gian Singh had no illusions about his personality. He was mad with anger. "You think every woman is running after your husband. What do you think your husband is, some kind of a Yousef? (He was alluding to the legendary hero of the Yousef-

Zulekha love story, the most handsome man of his time.) Have you seen your husband's face from a close range? Flies are scared of landing on his face; he is so ugly. A Scarecrow would have a better chance of seducing a woman than your hubby." Frothing at the mouth he went on and on.

Sushminder's anger had disappeared and was at first replaced by amazement at his eloquence and then by amusement at the way Gian was describing himself. As soon as he terminated his tirade, with a finger pointed at his face, she burst into laughter. She threw herself onto her bed and holding onto her aching sides she started rolling, unable to control her laughter.

Gian Singh stormed out of his home and went straight to the liquor store and bought a bottle of Solan # 1, his favorite. From there he proceeded to Sehaj Singh's home where he shared his whiskey and his sorrow with his bosom buddy.

"Did you actually say scarecrow?" Sehaj wanted to make sure.

"Yes, I am sure I used that word." Gian responded.

"Looking at you closely, I can see some resemblance." Sehaj teased him affectionately.

They sat together late into the night and polished off the bottle. Finally Gian got up relieved after having unburdened his sorrow.

"Good night," he said and turned to leave.

"Good night, Scarecrow," Sehaj shot back.

Not many people can say with any surety how Scarecrow got his name but it stuck to him like somebody had used a few tubes of Feviquick, whose formula, he would inform you, was stolen by the West and patented as Krazyglue. To argue that his statement was in conflict with the chronological order of the way things happened, Krazyglue having appeared in the Western markets years before anybody had heard about Feviquick, Scarecrow would insist, was like trying to skin a hair. He might even add that you can skin a hare but not a hair. Anyway, the date a formula is evolved has no relevance to the date the product is marketed. A formula may remain dormant for ages before the product hits the market. Yogis of yore are known to have passed on the ancient secret of the 'panacea' to their descendents only with their last breath in life. Obviously, due to some minute miscalculation with astronomical consequences the last one with the secret missed his chance to whisper the doomed formula into the ear of his descendent by one fateful breath otherwise someone would have it today. You have to give credit where credit is due. There is solid logic behind Scarecrow's line of reasoning.

You may not know Scarecrow's real name but if you do not know him well, you are certainly not from Moga, our laid-back town. Gian Singh's real name was not commonly known and was hardly ever used, except while addressing him, face to face.

Scarecrow was a smart fellow; had his wits around him, always. Always, though, even from that close range, he did not find it easy to locate them. But when he did make contact with his wits, he was a smart fellow. He was also a smart dresser. Whether he was in court appearing before the local magistrate or he went shopping, he was always seen dressed in his black jacket (coat, as it is generally known in India), black tie, white pants and a professionally starched and pressed white shirt, exactly as a lawyer should be dressed in a court. Of course, he must be wearing his underwear too but let us not get into that. And it is not suggested that you would have any intention of getting into his underwear if not counseled to refrain from it. Even out of court, in public he preferred to dress as a professional lawyer. It was his personal preference. Maybe he did not want the public in general to forget that he was licensed by the Government of India to practice law.

Nobody outside of his immediate family had ever seen him in casuals. One can only make a wild guess and venture to say that his wife must have seen him without his formal attire at least once, because among other things, he had a son. He did not have the other things in the same manner, though, as he had his son, it must be cleared.

I was busy with my small stationary store business one day when Scarecrow barged in.

"Why can't people leave me alone? Why, in the name of whatever it is, if anything, that is sacred to them, they can't leave me alone? Is it asking too much?" Going by the symptoms, Scarecrow was in an advanced stage of flusteration. (Don't reach for the dictionary, it is not there. It is a state of being flustered.)

It was a hot, humid day. I offered him a glass of cold water. He gulped down the refreshing liquid, took out a handkerchief from the pocket of his pants and wiped the perspiration off his face, giving his forehead a good scrub in the process.

"It is really hot today. The mercury must be hitting high forties," I was trying my best to calm him down.

"On top of everything else," was his terse remark.

"O yes, the humidity too is so oppressive; it is above ninety percent if anything," I made another effort to take his mind off what was bothering him.

There was a long awkward pause before he spoke, "You know why they can catch me so easily? It is because the river is thirty kilometers away." I had known all the time that it was coming. It was only a matter of time. Finally he started unloading the extra burden off his mind and yet I was none the wiser for it.

"The river?" I was only trying to hold onto my end of the conversation.

"Won't they have to travel that far to catch fish, if they were to catch fish instead?" It seemed so simple and straightforward to him. He and I speak the same language; Punjabi is our mother-tongue and yet he could have been speaking Latin and made no less sense to me.

My customer was no wiser on the subject of rivers and fish than I was. He took his mind off what he had come to buy and decided to expose his mind to some enlightenment.

"Of course; of course. Perhaps I was not paying attention." I apologized.

"You know Ganju, that fellow with the crooked left arm and with an equally crooked mind that sells fried fish at the corner down the street. He knows how difficult it is to catch fish. He spends practically the whole day catching fish that he sells in the evening. He charges his customers prices unheard of anywhere else. He is a daylight robber in the guise of a fried fish vendor, except that he carries on his extortion business well into the night too. But that is half the story. He serves illegally distilled country liquor and that too with police protection. On any given night you can see policemen on duty making seemingly casual stops at his joint but actually helping themselves to the fried fish and the booze. I know they never pay for the refreshments. Instead they bring him free country liquor. They never have to pay for it either. They can always manage to lift a few bottles out of the confiscated lots at the police station. Everybody seems to be comfortable with the arrangement. The fish vendor gets free booze to sell to honest citizens in need after the liquor stores close and the policemen get free fish. One hand, as they say, washes the other. You scratch my back; I'll scratch yours." Scarecrow had decided to give us a glimpse of the local underworld.

"Who pays for the booze that the policemen confiscate?" My customer's inquisitive mind was riding a dizzy tangent.

"I am a hardworking honest lawyer and not the head of an investigating agency. I have had my days in court, I have to say that. I know where the liquor comes from. Everybody knows where it comes from. It is an open secret. Who pays for it and who doesn't? I know I have to pay for it through the nose, that is, if I ever have to buy it from that thief. And you won't get it free either. You would have to cough up twice as much here as you would be required to pay at a half decent pub." Having worked out his anger, he felt a lot better. Coming generations of historians though will remain ignorant of the source of his initial indignation when he had stepped into my store.

Scarecrow and Sehaj Singh were very good friends. Sehaj Singh was in fact Gian Singh's only friend. People loved to meet Gian Singh but none except Sehaj Singh could stand him for long. They were both born and brought up in the same neighborhood as were their ancestors. Both had lived there all their lives. Both families owned sizeable tracts of agricultural land not too far from the town, which not too long ago was a rural community. Their main income was the revenues from these rural properties. If Gian Singh's family had to depend on the income from his law practice, they would be living below the poverty line, as defined by the Government of India.

Scarecrow's wife Sushminder was the Principal of a local Secondary school. Thcy had a son, Gurmeet, their only child. Sehaj Singh's wife was a homemaker. They had a daughter, Preet, their only child. Since she had been a baby, of all the children in the locality, Preet had been Gian Singh's favorite. He had loved her as his own child but had pampered her more than his own son. Like any other child, she loved being spoiled. As such she spent a lot of time sitting on his knee, playing with his beard. She spent more time in Scarecrow's home than in her own. Gurmeet was a couple of months older than Preet and had assumed the role of a protector.

But children's relationships have their ups and downs too. It was a typical day in the lives of the families: Gian was in his home when Gurmeet came in running and panting for breath and said urgently, "Daddy, come out, come out quickly." And he ran out as fast as he had come in.

"What is the matter, Son?" asked Gian, following his son dutifully.

When Gian came out of his home he saw Preet crying as if she was in mortal pain.

"What happened to my little angel?" Gian wanted to know as he approached her. But finding a sympathizer the child started crying even more loudly.

"Daddy, say sorry to her." Suggested Gurmeet.

"Why? What did I do?" Gian enquired of his son.

"Just say sorry and say it quickly. Can't you see she is hurt?" His son demanded.

"How did she get hurt?" Gian asked with visible concern.

"Can't you see? I kicked her." Said his son accusingly.

"Then why don't you say sorry?" Gian tried to reason with his son.

"Because." Gurmeet concluded his unquestionable argument.

Gian gave in and addressed Preet, "I am sorry, my darling angel."

In response the screaming child ran towards her own home screaming as loudly as her lungs would support.

"Look what you have done." Gurmeet shot at his father in disgust.

"I said sorry. Didn't I?" Gian tried to explain.

"But you didn't mean it." Gurmeet said as he too departed in the direction of Preet's home. He had his father's genes alright.

Tall like his mother, Gurmeet grew up to be a handsome young man. Preet turned out to be a good natured pretty young girl. Growing up together, they studied at the same institutions. It was quite natural for the children to marry each other when they grew up. The young couple believed they had married for love and the indulgent parents encouraged them to believe so. Things worked to everyone's satisfaction and the young couple had started living in Scarecrow's home.

Scarecrow never tired of reminding his friend that being the father of the boy he had a superior status and must therefore now be revered. Being the girl's father Sehaj must show him respect.

"Sure, sir. Why not." His friend would retort with mock obeisance.

The young couple once had a tiff over some trifling matter. Scarecrow sniffed it somehow. Without bothering to consult the contestants on the matter, he went huffing and puffing to Sehaj's home which was in the immediate vicinity. The young couple had no idea where he had gone.

"Is this how you raised your daughter?" Scarecrow shouted at his friend as soon as he was in sight.

"What did she do this time?" His friend was used to his outbursts. Being conscious that he was Scarecrow's only friend, he was quite considerate.

"Isn't that quite irrelevant to the situation? I haven't come here to discuss what she does or doesn't do. I am talking about her upbringing. Did you bring her up or pull her up by the ears? She used to be such a sweet child; look what you have made of her."

He had come to unburden his anger. He was in no mood to listen to any rubbish.

“And what has the sweet child become now?” asked his friend in his indulgent way.

“If you can stop pecking your wife for a change, maybe you can come and see for yourself.” Sehaj Singh’s wife was not so close to her husband but that was irrelevant to Scarecrow who turned homeward with his friend in toe.

“I am telling you, you can’t avoid the consequences. My son has had enough of it.” With these words he entered his home and flung open the door of his son’s room, inviting his friend to enter and examine the evidence firsthand.

His friend took one look inside and without a moment’s delay ran back to his own home covering his face with both hands.

And now it was Scarecrows turn to enter. His son and his son’s wife were not expecting any intrusion. Scarecrow’s wife was attending a parent-teacher meeting in her school. The young couple decided to give themselves an amorous evening. Gurmeet and Preet were not fully dressed. The young man had his wife in his lap and was feeding her grapes, one at a time, mouth to mouth. Preet was receiving the fruit with giggles of appreciation. Taken aback by the unexpected interruption the young man stood up clumsily letting go of his wife with a jolt that sent her rolling across the floor. Scarecrow turned his face the other way and started shouting insults at both of them but especially at his son whom he called henpecked among other things. The worst part of the episode was that he could hear peals of laughter coming from the direction of Sehaj Singh’s home.

Then there was the time when Scarecrow appeared in front of the magistrate representing a defendant who was charged by the Department of Wild Life with having shot down a couple of partridges out of season. The officials of the department had what is known as an open and shut case, or so they thought.

Scarecrow had a completely different picture of the case. He was not so much interested in proving that his client was innocent; that would be impossible. He was not even interested in proving that his client could not have broken the law. His only concern was to prove that the case against his client was built on probabilities; that no matter how remote the chances were, the possibility of his being innocent could not be completely ruled out. Scarecrow claimed that he could come up with numerous case scenarios in which his client would have to be innocent. He assured the court that he was in no way questioning the honesty and the integrity of the officials. He was only saying that they might have come to hasty conclusions.

"Suppose," he said, "that someone else had shot the birds and left them there. And that his client just picked them up as gifts from Providence."

"Now, why would someone shed innocent blood and then leave the meat there?" the magistrate wanted to know.

"Vegetarians do it all the time." Scarecrow had his wits around him.

"Thanks for educating me." The pliable magistrate offered no resistance.

"You are welcome, sir. First of all I did not say that it happened that way. I am taking a hypothetical stance here. According to the law of the land I do not have to prove my client's innocence. The onus is on the department of Wild Life to prove that he is guilty, beyond doubt." He argued.

"What was he doing with the birds? Why did he pick them up?" The court wanted satisfaction.

Scarecrow had a habit of going with the flow and had already forgotten about his assertion that his client had accepted them as gifts from Providence.

“Suppose he wanted to return the dead birds to the department. And I am not saying that he wanted to do that. We are talking about possibilities, so that we can rule out the ‘doubt factor’.”

“For what purpose would he want to return the dead birds to the department? What would they want to do with them?”

“That is a very relevant question, My Lord, though it is addressed to the wrong party, if I may be allowed to point out. I do not think the honorable officials would need my opinion on the subject of how best to deal with the dead birds but fowl goes well with red wine or vice versa, as is well known.”

Everyone in the court was amused.

“So in your opinion your client was only acting in the spirit of a conscientious citizen.” Seemingly the magistrate was being helpful.

“If he found the birds after their sad demise.” Scarecrow wanted to set the records straight.

“Any other possibilities?” The magistrate had a routine, boring, tiring day. He was enjoying himself.

“My client may have, unintentionally, of course, surprised the birds in the bush.” Scarecrow was getting into his rhythm. “Driven by fear and a will to survive one of the birds may have charged and unintentionally and quite accidentally may have squeezed with his claw the trigger of the shotgun in the hands of my client while its mate was trying to fly away from the danger zone. The gunshot may have found a target in the fleeing bird that happened to be at the wrong place at the wrong time, as is generally said on such occasions."

"Any theory about how the second bird died?" The magistrate was now thinking of how he was going to entertain his family that evening.

"The same way as the first bird died. What is good for the duck is good for the drake." Scarecrow seemed to have wound up the case satisfactorily.

"But the first bird was shot dead by the second bird. Are you suggesting that the dead bird suddenly got up and shot down the second bird?" The magistrate was incredulous. He had known Scarecrow for quite some time but this was too much even for him.

"It could have happened simultaneously, Your Honor." Scarecrow was not known for giving up but even he found the going a bit rough. He quickly changed his stance and suggested, "Struck by remorse and refusing to live without his partner, the second bird may have decided to put an end to his own miserable lonely life."

"Do you mean the second bird could have committed suicide?" The magistrate was now at the end of his tether.

"Swans are known to do it all the time, I mean if their partner dies." Scarecrow clarified.

"But we are talking about partridges."

"If a crow can learn how to walk like a swan, Your Honor, a partridge surely can learn to die like a swan." Scarecrow was quite emphatic in his assertion.

It was too much to take. He threw his head back as a guffaw escaped the magistrate's wide open mouth. The courtroom seemed to explode as everyone present, including the officials of the department, burst into uncontrollable laughter. There was a slight exchange of signals between the magistrate and the officials and he threw up his hands and threw the case out.

*****

The Odd Worm

Like puppets on the stage
Of life we dance to the
Recorded tunes of destiny
With the zest of creative choreographers
Cherishing hopes
For the final selection to dance
In the ballet-eternal though
The selection had been made
Before time began ticking.

The disciple had finished his routine chores, had served his mystic master his last meal of the day and was sitting at his feet enjoying the holy bliss of being within his spiritual aura.

You could not hazard a guess of the age of the ancient master except to say that he was very old. His snow-white long flowing beard covered most of his face, barely sparing the nose. His bushy drooping eyebrows were shielding his eyes. And yet he did not have the withered look of old age. Instead his face glowed with a divine saintly aura. His eyes shone with compassionate universal love. Anyone looking into those eyes would be drawn by a fatherly affection.

The disciple had been engaged in the service of his master for over a decade but the master had initiated him onto the spiritual path only recently. Since his initiation, the disciple's curiosity regarding the secrets of mysticism had shot up quite a few notches. Among other things, he wanted to know about his future here on earth but more so hereafter. The present, the master would explain, is where we are reading history not knowing what the following pages contain. But the book has been written, its details running into eternity. Notwithstanding the master's assurance that all his queries would be resolved automatically as he made spiritual progress within himself, he kept pestering his master with various kinds of questions. The master tried to satisfy his curiosity while at the same time he wanted his disciple to understand that in order to be able to relate to the answers to his questions he would need to have attained some degree of spiritual progress within himself, without which the answers would make little sense to him. And yet the questions kept coming.

Even stronger was the disciple's curiosity about his master. The disciple had known that his master was an army veteran who lived off his pension and that he had been the disciple of a perfect saint of his day. He was also conscious of the fact that his master loved him like he was his own son. But that was the extent of his knowledge. The disciple was not so much interested in knowing who his master was as he was keen to know what he was. Was he just a well meaning compassionate person overflowing with the milk of human kindness or was he something more than a human being, some superior being, someone divinely blessed, a demigod or someone still greater than that? The disciple often wondered. He was aware that the answer to this question would never come from his master. And he knew no other means of finding out.

Drunk with the divine love that was flowing from his master's presence the disciple asked his master, "Master, I have heard you speak about marked souls, being souls destined to attain salvation. What is a marked soul? How is it different from the rest of humanity?"

The mystic closed his eyes and remained silent for a considerable spell as if he was consulting a Higher Authority for the most appropriate answer to the disciple's question.

Slowly, the mystic master opened his eyes and addressed his disciple: "Son, I am going to unravel the secret for you, do have the patience to listen to it."

"I am all ears, Master," responded the eager disciple.

The master started the story thus:

"Before the beginning of time, there was God and nothing but God. There were no stars, no sun, no moon and no earth. There was nothing except God; not even the space between the heavenly bodies. The universe had not yet come into being. There was no light, not even the void waiting to be filled in.

Then for reasons best known to Him, God decided to bring about the creation. Since there was nothing in existence except God, He had to create the creation out of Himself. So God uttered one explosive Sound and the entire creation in its primitive form came into being.

Having created the physical universe, God decided to populate it by creating living beings. Living beings need souls to be alive. So God created souls out of His own being. Naturally the souls were exactly like God except that they were on a much smaller scale. You can say that each soul was God in miniature. God was infinite, so were the souls. God was all love and light, so were the souls, on a much smaller scale, of course.

When God told the souls in His nonverbal divine language that they were being sent into the creation to populate it, they were excited about it. They were going on an excursion, they thought. It felt like starting on an adventure. They danced about joyfully at the prospect of wearing bodies. The possibilities, they thought, were simply limitless.

But not all souls were happy at the prospect of emerging out of God and going into the creation. These souls said to God, in the same divine language, of course, that they did not want to be a part of the creation; they would much rather remain a part of the Creator in eternal bliss as before. These latter, my Son are the marked souls.

The souls that were happy to leave God and become a part of the creation are to remain a part of the creation for ever, passing through one life form to another. They shall revolve in the cycle of 8.4 million types of life forms without ever a chance of escape. This process of birth and death, of the soul shifting from one body to another you already know is called transmigration of the soul.

God promised to the souls that never wanted to leave Him that they would be called back to be with Him and to merge with Him never to separate again.

'I will send my emissaries to the world from time to time to bring back these marked souls to me. They will then be, for all eternity, indistinguishable from me; they will be God as they have been before creation.' God promised to these souls.

The disciple asked his master, "Master, how will the marked souls find their way back to God?"

"God sends His emissaries in the form of saints, God realized souls, to find and bring back all these souls; not one marked soul will be left behind. When a marked soul is ready to make the journey back to God, the emissary will appear. Such, my dear Son, is the divine law."

"Master, how will a marked soul recognise an emissary?"

"The emissary, let us call him a 'saint', will recognise all the marked souls allotted to him by God. The soul that returns to God and merges with Him becomes God to remain in eternal bliss. Just as a rain drop falls into the ocean and becomes the ocean. This is called emancipation or salvation of the soul."

"So that is why you found me, Master. I am a marked soul allotted to you by God and you are taking me back to Him, are you not, Master?"

"You, my Son, are a marked soul and you are going back to God as I am. I am going to tell you another story." said the Master and proceeded thus:

Among the thicket of a forest, lived countless worms. There were all kinds of worms. Some were short, others were long. They came in all colours. There was a large variety of worms. But one thing was common to all the worms. They all loved filth. That is why they lived in the muddiest, the slimiest and the smelliest part of the forest. They enjoyed it there. The mulch was simply heavenly. They loved the warmth and the softness of the earth. Their food was so plentiful, they practically lived in it. Earth is what they thrived on. To crown it all, there was no shortage of other worms to rub their backs against. The place was teeming with the slithery slimy creatures. Rubbing backs against one another was the favourite pastime of the worms. When they were not eating filth, they were rubbing backs against one another. They simply could not stop doing it. You can say it was their second nature and you would not be wrong. It gave them immense pleasure to indulge in this manner.

The worms did not call their thicket 'the Garden of Eden'. They had never heard of a place with such a name. They would certainly have given their part of the forest this name, if only they had known what it meant. In the truest sense this was the worms' Garden of Eden.

But then there was this odd worm. He was a worm among worms but an odd one; odd to the point that he refused to join the fun of rubbing backs. In other words he simply refused to have a good time. While all the worms loved to dig into the dark, moist recesses of the earth, which happens to be the age old, respected conduct of the wormdom, the odd one climbed trees.

Among the not-so-few oddities of this strange worm, and topping all the rest, was his claim to, what he called "sight".

"Sight!" giggled the worms, curling three-fold with mirth.

"Yes, I have sight", asserted the odd worm.

"And how do you play with what you have?" asked a lively one.

"I see with it", said the worm that claimed to have sight.

The gathered worms were really enjoying themselves now. They doubled with laughter; they tripled with laughter.

"Yes, I see. I see the bright sun. I see the beautiful colours of the flowers. I see the birds and the animals in the forest. Furthermore, I can see you living in filth", went on this unique creature to the collective merriment of the multitude as the worms were revelling in, what this one called filth.

Try as he would, there was no way this odd worm could communicate to the sightless creatures what sight was and what powers it was capable of bestowing on the blessed one who possessed it. In this situation their handicap was as much his own in so far as he failed to explain the difference between them and himself. Even if he had a way of impressing upon the worms that they were miserably handicapped, it would serve no one. They were what they were and he was what he was and nothing would change that.

Suddenly, one day, this odd worm was overpowered by a nauseating feeling of disgust with his life among these worms. And the very next moment he was filled with a blissful sensation, the like of which he had never felt before.

"Hey!" He shouted, "I am not one of you. I am different. I am totally different from you. I am not even a worm.

He started exerting against what he had known to be his skin. He pushed and he wriggled. He wriggled and he pushed. The crusty shell that had imprisoned him fell off and he emerged from it bearing a pair of magnificent and the most beautifully coloured wings.

In the bright sunlight he took off and soon found himself surrounded by other majestically winged creatures like himself. He not only had sight but flight too. He discovered, in his state of rapture, that he was a butterfly. He was not a worm. He never was. The memories of the worms, like unpleasant dreams, already receding into oblivion, he headed straight towards the source of light.

“That, my Son, is the end of the story. If you have no more questions, then we shall put on hold our discussion till tomorrow.”

“There is one question that has been bothering me for some time, Master. Will I ever learn to love you the way you love me?”

“During the course of your spiritual journey, Son, you shall attain a stage where you will stop thinking of yourself as a body that has a soul in it; you will then realize that your real self is a soul that wears an expendable, disposable body and that you have worn and discarded million of bodies before you came to don your present body. Now you think of yourself as a human being who is seeking spiritual experience. A stage will come in your spiritual odyssey Son, when you will finally realize that you are in fact a spiritual being who is going through a human experience.

“Then you will also come to realize that all living beings are also souls wearing various kinds of bodies. At that stage you will be able to see all other beings as souls, exactly like yourself with no distinguishing marks at all. Then you will not be able to distinguish one from the other; nor will you be able to distinguish between yourself and other souls. All souls being exactly identical like drops from the same divine ocean, sparks of the same divine refulgence, you will love all other souls as you love yourself and it will be effortless, spontaneous love. You will not be able to help loving all souls and that includes me, my Son.”

“When, my Master, when?”

“This my Son, is the greatest adventure that a soul separated from its Source will ever undertake. Patience and perseverance are qualities you will have to cultivate for this adventure of all adventures. The answer to your question is: In the fullness of time a mango drops from the tree. It cannot drop a moment earlier and it cannot stay attached to the tree a moment longer. When the time is ripe a baby is born. It cannot be born a moment earlier and it cannot stay in the womb of its mother one moment longer.

In the fullness of time, Son, no sooner and no later.
And remember that our destiny was writ before time started ticking.”

*****

A Matter of Urgency

Sunder and Radha Malhotra were the happiest couple I had ever known. During the twenty five odd years of their marriage there was hardly anyone who had ever seen one of them without the other. They were inseparable. If looks could be depended upon, they were absolutely madly in love with each other all through their married life. And then Radha died. I received an e-mail explaining how she died of a massive cardiac arrest. Hospitals in Nova Scotia, Canada are perpetually heavily booked and her waiting period for a bypass surgery proved to be one day too long. She was scheduled to be operated upon the next day. I was shocked. Without knowing how to console Sunder I called and laid down the usual stuff; how we cannot fight destiny so we must bow down to the inevitable and accept the writ as the will of the Lord. He wept profusely and sounded confused and disoriented. Their young son Naveen who lived in Vancouver came and stayed with his father for a week before returning to his research work at the UBC. I kept calling Sunder regularly and I tried to cheer him up the best I could.

Then almost a month after the tragic death of my friend's wife, I got a phone call from him in the middle of the day. I was at my office in the Khan Market, New Delhi. I realized it was almost midnight in Halifax.

"I need to get married." He said.

"Why would you want to get married so soon after the death of dear Radha?" It seemed so insensitive of him. I failed to understand him. It was not like him at all.

"I didn't say I want to get married. I need to get married." He corrected me. I was perplexed to put it mildly.

‘Oh my God!’ I said to myself.

“But why the urgency? Have you got some unsuspecting woman in trouble?” I spoke without thinking because to find that out he would need far more than a month.

“It’s nothing of the sort. I am not that type of a man and you know that well.” He assured me.

“Then what compels you to get married now; considering your age?

“It’s got nothing to do with age.”

“Will you keep me guessing or will you let me know exactly what the matter is.” I was losing my patience.

“I forgot to stop taking the pills.” He tried to put it succinctly in his own way.

“What pills?” I was none the wiser for his statement.

“The ginseng and ….” He started enlightening me. But I cut him short.

“Well that’s an original. I have heard of people forgetting to take their pills but forgetting to stop taking pills, I did not know it could happen. Are you now telling me that you were taking sexual potency enhancing pills after your wife died? But why? Everything we do has to have some logic behind it.” I was furious by now.

“I don’t know; force of habit, I guess.” He was talking like he had been caught being naughty in his primary school days and that he was trying to explain to his Headmistress.

“Well stop now.” I almost shouted into the phone.

"It won't help now. Lately, I have not been behaving rationally. Radha has left me in a bewildered state."

Sunder was in a bad shape. Despite the seemingly comic situation in which he had landed himself his condition was pitiable and needed immediate help. The gist of what he explained to me was that kicking and bucking on the heels of hefty doses of the Siberian ginseng in his system, that he had been increasing steadily over the years, a sizeable build up of the most potent of the Indian drugs, *Shilajeet* in his testosterone manufacturing units was screaming for immediate release and for the registry of its volcanic forebodings.

"There is more. I haven't told you everything Jeevan, you can appreciate that I have been so lonely." He continued rather apologetically.

"It is quite natural for you to feel lonely after the death of dear Radha. There is nothing unusual about it. Anyone in your situation would feel lonely." I tried to cheer him up.

"It is not so easy to explain. I feel like I am sitting on top of a live volcano. I don't know how to say it." He hesitated and before he could go on I encouraged him to speak his mind.

"Just say it as it is Sunder, there is nothing that you can tell me that I won't understand." I assured him.

"I have been watching blue films." He blurted out. I had spoken too soon, I realized. I was trying to adjust my reaction to his bizarre statement. I could not determine whether to laugh or lose my temper. Reflexively, boiling anger took over and I felt I was losing control of myself.

"But why, you idiot? You are supposed to be a rational human being. Like a blasted fool, you have been helping yourself to appetizers and boosting your hunger for the food that you do not have."

"Jeevan, I am miserably lonely. I don't know what to do with myself."

"Try to stay busy with your work. That will take care of your days." I tried to regain my calm sympathetic composure.

"It is not the days that pose the most serious problem. Jeev, may I come to you?" He pleaded.

"You want to come to India? How is that going to solve your problem?" I had no idea what he was implying.

"Where else can I go? You are my only dependable friend in times of need." More than anything else he seemed to be in dire need of a shoulder to cry on. At least that is what I thought he was asking for.

"But you can't neglect your business indefinitely. Ultimately you will have to go back to Canada." He was running a chain of successful pizza outlets.

"Right now I am least concerned with the 'ultimately'. You know I am not the type who will go sleeping around. I have always maintained very high moral standards. I have never crossed the bounds of decency. What I need is a wife." He prioritized his need.

"But you don't have a wife." I wanted him to wake up to the realty.

"That is the problem and that is why I want to come to you."

"I do not mind your coming to me, in fact I would love to be with you now more than ever. What I do not understand is the way you somehow seem to relate me to your need for a wife."

"India is the ideal place for me at this time. In Canada I am quite handicapped. Here you have to keep dating someone indefinitely before you can pose the question of wedlock and I cannot afford that luxury. Time is what I don't have. Also most Canadian women would like to 'know you intimately' before agreeing to marry you. You know what I mean. I consider that grossly immoral. Not that I have something to hide. There is nothing wrong with me. The only thing that is wrong with me is that I cannot wait. I hope you understand what I am saying." He entreated.

Finally, I understood only too well. He had pushed himself into a sweet jam. And I realized that he had a very valid point. And yet I could not agree with him that India in any way offered a solution to his problems.

"I need a wife and I need her fast. In India it is customary to ask a stranger to marry you. All you need is a matchmaker, a sort of a go-between. And you are there for me. Ain't you Jeev?" He implored.

"You are quite right about arranged marriages. They are still prevalent in this country. And you are my very dear friend Sunder but I am no good at matchmaking. I have no experience." I tried to explain to him.

"You can find one who is good at it Jeev, I should have consulted you first, I know but I have already booked a flight for India. I am sorry it is a bit of a surprise but I am landing at the IGI Airport on the eleventh of this month." That was less than a week away. And he started giving me the details of his travel itinerary.

The flight arrived on schedule. Dressed in an impeccable dark brown suit he came and gave me a bear hug holding and squeezing me like he was afraid to let go. I hugged him equally warmly and extricating myself from his hold a little awkwardly grabbed his baggage cart that he had pushed aside to meet me. We exchanged pleasantries as we walked making slow progress through the throng of passengers looking for their loved ones or seeking means of transport. Travel and hotel agents were pushing and shoving to get your attention. Taxi drivers were trying to snatch your baggage cart from you. I loaded the baggage in the trunk of my car and dropped the cart at the trolley corral.

On the way home I tried to avoid the topic of his matrimonial prospects. Once at home he was glad to meet Urmila, my wife. Guddu and Pinky, our children were at school. We went into the living room and Urmila got busy in the kitchen preparing tea for us. Before his bottom hit the chesterfield, Sunder posed the inevitable question, “Have you made the arrangements?”

I was not sure what he expected me to have accomplished before his arrival. “The only course of action for people in our situation is to advertise in the matrimonial columns of the local newspapers and wait for the results.” I offered as an opinion.

“And have you done that?” he asked eagerly.

“I couldn’t do that without consulting you.”

“What is there to consult? All I want is a lady willing to marry me. Isn’t that obvious?”

“But what are your expectations? What do you expect your future wife to be like? Only you can decide that.”

He was exasperated. “A female of the human species with body parts intact: The one who will say yes when I ask her to marry me. There is nothing complicated about it.” He said it with pronounced irritability.

“Sunder, you intend to spend the rest of your life with this person. You must know her tastes, her likes and dislikes, her family and cultural background, her education. You can’t just pick anyone who suddenly pops up out of nowhere. She quite possibly will be the mother of your future children. There is a whole lot to be considered.” I wanted him to calm down and proceed cautiously.

"Let's place the ad then. If we mail the ads, they will send us the bills to be paid in advance and then we will make the payments through mail. That could take forever before the ads reach the readers. I suggest we write the ad and deliver it to the offices of all the major dailies in the city personally and make the payments at the counter. This will save us all the time and trouble." He was being practical.

"Can we have tea first?" I enquired.

"You can spare the sarcasm, Jeev, my bro. If it hadn't been a matter of urgency, I wouldn't have put you through all this hassle." He was sounding diplomatic.

In response to our ads while scores of prospective brides applied through mail, as we were to find out later, Ranjana came in person wheeling her suit case behind her. Like Sunder she also did not believe in wasting time. She would not be the one who sat at home waiting for the mailman to knock while the trophy had been snatched away by an enterprising competitor. Her home was not too far away, she told us. Then why the suit case? Her attitude was shocking to say the least. It would be considered scandalous in any civilised society but considering this was India, it was absolutely unacceptable and unladylike. If the news got around, headlines in the gossip columns of the local tabloids would scream shame and that would be disastrous for the girl. It would do no good to my and my family's reputation.

She explained at length that she had defied her parents in leaving her home and coming like this and that she was not going back. Sunder, mellow-eyed and enchanted was hanging on to every word she spoke and something seemed to have clicked between them while she was talking about her irreversible decision. And since she had declared she was not going back home and also since Sunder was in no mood to throw her out I decided to put her up in the spare bedroom for the night on the condition that she would immediately call her parents and inform them of her whereabouts. I would not want the police to be looking for her.

Our children wanted to know who the 'Auntie' was. We tried to explain that she was a friend of Sunder Uncle and had come to see him. We knew they were not impressed and they knew that we knew. They were whispering to each other continuously. I think they knew exactly what she was there for.

A long conversation took place between Urmila and me during the night. If I had been looking for an ideal bride for Sunder, which I was, I would have rejected Ranjana offhand. Urmila saw things differently. She was not talking about the ideal but the ideally suited. So I climbed down from the ideal to the presentable. Urmila admonished me, "If he can present himself in a certain society, he can damn well present her too. He may be your dearest friend but he is no Prince Charming himself." I did not think she had a valid point. I emphasized that Sunder should choose the most eligible of those who would want to marry him. Urmila was not convinced. "By the way, for whom are you selecting a wife, for him or for yourself? And bear in mind he needs someone who can physically cope with his habit of 'forgetting to stop pill-popping' and not someone with a twenty five inch waist." Urmila had a point there. May be I was getting too emotionally involved in this matter of selection.

"Look at him and look at the way he is looking at her." Urmila went on. And Sunder was the beholder who had an eye stuffed to choking with beauty. He had been eyeing Ranjana with a gleam in his eyes that outshone the look my snow-white German shepherd Argus had when he looked at a chicken leg. "It is Sunder who must have the final say in this matter." Urmila put her foot firmly down. I began to wonder, 'Was Urmila trying to get rid of the problem by short-selling my bosom buddy?'

It is of vital interest not only to the prospective bride groom but also to the reader to know the age of the bride-to-be. In the case of

Ranjana it is important to state that she belonged to a multiple set of age groups starting from the late twenties and going up the scale to the late thirties and beyond depending on whether you met her in the early evening when she was freshly made up or early morning when serious cracks had appeared in the facial plaster screaming for urgent repair work. For our purpose, we will label her age as 'nondescript' and leave it at that. Not bad, Urmila suggested, considering our hero was heading fast toward fifty. He wasn't qualified to marry what is popularly known as a spring chicken.

Ranjana certainly was not fat. She was built on the lines of a Russian auto factory worker with the kind of bottom on which the sun never sets. If she were in a tug of war competition, you would have no hesitation placing her at the rear end of the team with the rope securely tied around her ample waist. Having secured it thus you would be safe as having your boat tied firmly at the mooring without any fear of it drifting away. Now beauty is an exceptionally subjective concept. Comparatively speaking, if you accept Helen of Troy as your standard model of beauty, you might as well dump the entire female population of the world as ugly, barring a stray Angelina Jolie or a rare Aishwariya Rai.

Ranjana made it clear to us that she was aware of her shortcomings and that she was advancing in years, well past the marriageable age for an Indian woman. She wanted to be considered, she pleaded, on compassionate grounds. If she were to deal with rejection this time she would have no option but to put an end to her miserable life. She expressed all this without any trace of malice.

There is no way you could call the woman under our scanner ugly. She had the face that in pleasant circumstances would belong to a very happy person. It had congeniality written all over it. Corkscrew curls that were the craze with Bollywood actresses of the sixties/seventies as they sang doleful songs holding on to tree trunks for support, were springing at the sides of her face. If I could afford a plastic surgeon for minor adjustments, which I could not, I would have asked him to lift the bridge of her nose a wee bit and chisel it on the sides. That would make it fit for a Roman princess to flaunt proudly in the coliseum where a dozen Christians were being fed to the hungry African lions. Then I would have asked the surgeon to adjust the rest of the face to go with the nose. A simple operation. Reminds me of my college days.

I needed a pair of shoes badly and money was in short supply. This was when a friend informed me that he had discovered a cobbler who could replace the entire worn out soles of your old shoes for three rupees. (We are talking about the good old mid forties, God 'RIP' them.) And if your big toe was sticking out of your shoe, this cobbler could replace the entire tops for five rupees. I was so exited I skipped my lunch, picked up my rickety, squeaky bicycle and rode out to the cobbler. Still out of breath, I asked the cobbler, "Uncle, I hear that you can replace the soles on a pair of shoes for three rupees and put up whole new tops for five rupees."

"You have heard it right, son."

"Uncle, please make a pair of soles and a pair of tops for me and I have the eight rupees for you."

"Son, I need a pair of your old shoes to start with."

"But a pair of shoes is what I do not have." I offered apologetically.

He looked pitiably at the half a rupee worth of the V shaped chappals (sandals) I was wearing and said, "You cannot have a new pair of shoes for eight rupees. That will cost you at least fifteen." Money in those days was hard to come by and I was passing through a period of particularly strained pecuniary circumstances. I neither had an old pair of shoes nor the sum of fifteen rupees to spare.

There is hardly any relevance and I don't know why but looking at her face I was reminded of that little episode. There was a marked difference because we did have the old face to start working on, that is, if I could afford a plastic surgeon, which I could not.

She had a set of pearly white regular teeth but you could not go ahead and ask her if they were her own. Anyway she could not be lying if she asserted that they were her own in case they were duly paid for by her. My wife pinched my ear jovially and told me to stop putting the lady down. Urmila put our minds at rest by declaring that her teeth were real and that they were beautiful.

At five foot two and a half and seventy two kg Sunder was short and stocky. With his cheeks hanging low he had a squarish face with a St. Bernard look. It would be easy to frame this face without leaving many empty spaces around. There were prominent dark bags under his eyes. With a haggard look on his face, he appeared far older than his years, the result of over indulgence, may be.

In the evening I was assisting Urmila in the kitchen when we heard a peal of laughter coming from the living room. I came out of the kitchen and saw that Sunder had cornered Ranjana against the wall. He had his hands on the wall with her between his arms. "I love you, I love you, I love you." His temples pulsating with passion, he was going on like the needle was stuck in one groove on the gramophone record. She was enjoying herself thoroughly. I informed Urmila about what was going on.

"You have to put a stop to the love-feast. The situation, with your friend in an overcharged state of excitement could get out of hand. Don't forget that we have children at home. Go and announce that dinner is ready." Urmila was seething with anger.

She was right too. He was behaving like a stag in rut who had beaten all his rivals in the neighborhood and having fairly and squarely earned the singular access to the harem had now cornered the prize impala who was in an obliging mood. His progress was marred only by the circumstance of their being in a family situation and perhaps by his own brand of a doubtful morality.

"Jeev Uncle, I can't have my dinner yet. I haven't done my *paath puja*." Ranjana addressed me. I am younger, not by much but younger all the same than my friend, her intended husband.

She may have noticed that we were a devoutly religious family. I am not absolutely sure the exercise was not meant to impress us. She must also have realized that I had a significant influence with Sunder.

Sure enough, she went and sat cross-legged on the carpet in a corner and started reciting the holy scriptures from memory. She went on and on reciting in flawless Sanskrit. I must admit I was impressed. She could not possibly have made that preparation overnight.

The next day in the in the presence of her family and some of our friends a hastily arranged wedding ceremony was performed. We prepared a room farthest from the children's rooms for them to stay while they waited for Ranjana's emigration papers to be completed. Sunder and Ranjana had some kind of chemistry between them. They were all over each other almost all the time. Both of them thanked us profusely for bringing them together.

We saw them off at the Indira Gandhi International Airport. They were headed for Canada for a loving, fulfilling, fruitful future. If her physique and his hunger for her physique were any indication, at least the fulfilling part was assured. To the inconvenience of the other passengers on board one of the washrooms on the flight could be occupied overtime.

*****

A Family Affair

Niranjan Dass instructed his legal secretary Preeti to ask the driver to bring the car around and told her that she was accompanying him on a visit to the Ahujas' residence in Greater Kailash. Accordingly, Preeti called Surjeet on his cell phone and repeated the instructions. Surjeet was ready in the driver's seat of the Mitsubishi Lancer at the front gate when Niranjan and Preeti emerged from the old building in Darya Ganj. Niranjan gave Surjeet the directions and started acquainting Preeti with the bare essentials of the Ahuja vs. Ahuja case.

The taxi radio was on giving news about the political scene in India. The opposition was attacking Manmohan Singh for being the weakest Indian Prime Minister ever. He had such a soft voice. It was more suited for singing nursery rhymes to tiny tots in a nursery school than for the tough office that he held. No matter how hard he tried the poor man could not even slightly froth at the mouth while delivering a speech from the Red Fort on Republic Day. His biggest problem was he never even tried. He could go on and on reading his scripted speech without ever flourishing his arms belligerently, completely ignoring that the country was surrounded by hostile forces and the enemy was on the alert watching his every move. But there was hardly any 'move' on his part. He is not only supposed to be belligerent, he should act and be seen as being belligerent. They doubted whether he could so much as spell 'belligerence' even if allowed to consult a dictionary. There were hordes of men and women eager to replace him who could literally set the nation ablaze just by opening their mouths. And they had credentials to prove their worth. In a glaring contrast, the Prime Minister could perhaps not even light a birthday candle given a dozen matchsticks.

Niranjan Dass, willowy five-foot-eleven, MA, LLB owned a compact but successful law firm and it took all the time he could devote to keep it on track and running smoothly like a well oiled machine. Manoj Sahiwal, his junior lawyer had been with him for a couple of years now. Some other fresh law graduates had joined the firm at different times but unable to cope with Niranjan's workaholic temperament and his excessive demands on their time had quit after short periods.

After graduating from the law college, this was Manoj's first job. Young and enthusiastic he was determined to succeed. He was sharp witted with a remarkable presence of mind. He was aggressive in the court. His only handicap was his inexperience and his dramatic approach was a bit raw around the edges. He needed to learn what only years of courtroom bouts can teach a young lawyer of his potential. He was normally looked upon as a future pillar of our legal structure.

Ravi Ahuja, his father Laxman and his mother Shanti had been emphatic in their statements that Ravi's wife Saroj had slipped from the top of the stairs and the head injury as shown in the medical report was the result of that fall down the stairs. Saroj, assisted by her parents had sued Ravi and his mother claiming that she was the victim of physical abuse at the hands of her husband and his mother and that even after a year of her marriage demands for dowry were showing no signs of subsiding. The fall, she claimed was the result of a deliberate push by her husband and that he had been instigated by his mother.

Ravi Ahuja wanted to retain Niranjan Dass to represent him in this case. Niranjan, a conscientious lawyer, wanted to ascertain first hand the plausibility of his case. Preeti would be an asset on this assignment not only to take notes but also to use her instincts as a young female and to don Saroj's shoes, as it were, and view the scenario from where she would stand.

During a protracted session of probing questions and answers also attended by Ravi's parents, Niranjan Dass, in his bid to find the truth of the matter, suggested to Ravi Ahuja, "Suppose we make the plea that you bumped into your wife accidentally at the top of the stairs causing her fall down the stairs, the plaintiff will still have to prove that you had intention of harming her and proving intentions is not easy. You will still have a fairly sound defence." But Ravi insisted that he was nowhere near her when his wife tumbled down the stairs.

"What could be the motive of your wife in accusing you if you were not involved in the accident in any way?" Niranjan Dass was curious to know.

"Mr Dass, there is no denying the fact that my relations with my wife are not ideally cordial. Obviously she is bent upon damaging my reputation and she will do her best to put me behind bars if she possibly can." Ravi Ahuja offered as an explanation.

"You have vehemently denied any demands of dowry by your family and I would like to believe you. What then is the real bone of contention? How did it all start? There has to be something substantial to cause this kind of a rift between your wife and the rest of your family." Niranjan wanted to know.

"Saroj is a very independent kind of a person. She is used to having her way in every situation. In a joint family like ours where we live with our parents, it is not always possible. There has to be some give and take. One has to show some respect and regard for the opinions and feeling of others. My wife is totally incapable of understanding and appreciating that simple rule." Ravi explained.

"Have you considered divorce? Please do not misunderstand me. I am not in any way suggesting that you should. I am keen on knowing how you feel about it."

"As soon as I am out of the present mess, I am filing for divorce, that is if she does not beat me to it." Ravi sounded quite determined.

"I must warn you Ravi that you will have to face some tough questions from your wife's counsel in the court room. It is quite natural for the court to be sympathetic towards the so called victim. People are normally prejudiced against those they believe to be guilty of family violence. Even before the case is under way you will be seen as a cruel person and your wife will be viewed as an oppressed victim. The media has not been very sympathetic to you and you are aware of it. It may turn out to be a nasty battle so you will have to prepare yourself for any eventuality. I am not trying to scare you. I am trying to prepare you for what lies ahead." Niranjan paused to make sure that the reality sinks in.

Then he continued, "Please make sure that you tell me everything that I must know before we go to court. I don't want to find out some awkward truths in cross examination. So I would request you in your own interest not to hide anything from me. I will hate to see your wife's counsel springing surprises in your face in the court. If you decide to change your story you can get in touch with me anytime before we go to court. I must also inform you now that if you change your stance under pressure from the other side during the course of the case, our firm shall have the option of withdrawing as your defence counsel." Niranjan Dass explained the terms clearly.

Niranjan Dass decided that he could take Ravi and his mother on their word and that Manoj, who would handle the case more or less independently, would be asked to contact the family and take up the defence proceedings. Ravi insisted that Niranjan should conduct the case himself and that he would not at all mind paying extra for that privilege but Niranjan explained that the workload of his previous commitments would not permit him to spare the time but that he would be glad to supervise and instruct Manoj as the case proceeded.

Satisfied at having disposed off that engagement as successfully concluded Niranjan took his leave and accompanied by Preeti emerged from the Ahuja mansion. Surjeet was waiting for them and they drove back to their office building.

It was closing time for the law office and Niranjan decided judiciously in favour of a taxi for his next trip. Again Preeti was to accompany him. The taxi came to a screeching halt in response Niranjan's signal. He held the door to the back seat open for Preeti to get in. Having instructed the cabbie to take them to Connaught Place, he settled down for the short trip. Without wasting any time the young cabbie, who looked like he could do with a serious scrub and wash, trained his rear view mirror at Preeti's face and gazed hopelessly at her whenever the traffic permitted. Going round the Place Niranjan asked the cabdriver to stop past an intersection and the taxi came to a stop. Niranjan paid the driver allowing him a tip that put a smile on his face.

Niranjan never learnt to drive and he did not want to bring his driver along. He was not the scheming type but a little bit of discretion was, he thought, in order. Anyway a taxi saved you the hassle of having to secure a difficult to find parking spot in the evening rush hours in this hub of New Delhi.

Dressed in his neatly pressed pinstripe dark blue suit Niranjan stepped out of the taxi holding the door open for Preeti. Preeti, a slender supple girl, was the kind of petite beauty that could take your breath away. She was casually dressed in a Punjabi style pale pink flowered kameez and shalwar in plain matching colour. She had a dupatta hanging back over her shoulders.

Out of the cab they merged into the exhilarating hustle and bustle of the evening Connaught Place crowd. Niranjan took her by the hand and guided her through the throng and into the dining area of his favourite haunt. Niranjan let go of her hand at the high double door entrance. The restaurant was almost full to capacity. This was the hour when late workers emerged from office complexes to seek refreshment. This was also the time when early diners headed for popular eating places. Those who planned on having a night on the town also needed an early bite before they could hit the night clubs and bars. This was a busy time for restaurants. Waiters and waitresses were weaving their way through the tables balancing plates in both hands above their heads.

Preeti followed him. The place had very few unoccupied tables. The restaurant was abuzz with people chatting at their tables. Preeti managed to turn a few heads as she made her entrance behind her boss. Niranjan did not wait to be guided to a table by a waiter. He went around to the bottom of the stairwell and looked back to make sure Preeti was not too far behind. She felt quite awkward walking behind, what seemed to her, an old man in such a place. She did not want to be seen with him like a couple and then again she did not want to give the impression that she was there against her will. He started climbing the steps leisurely with Preeti following at a respectable distance. He was no stranger to the place and seemed to know his way around. This was Preeti's first visit to the House. In fact this was the first time she had been inside a place that looked so exclusive to her. She could not have afforded a meal at a restaurant of this class on her week's wages.

At the landing of the upper floor the waiter gave Niranjan an understanding smile. He seemed to be pretty sure that the man would not care much for a view of the street or the park beyond so he led them to a neatly appointed little cabin in an alcove towards the back of the building. There was a table set for two. This was Niranjan's first outing with this timid girl. He guided her to one of the chairs and took the seat opposite her.

Niranjan was very fond of this slip of a girl. Apart from being a lovable person she was very useful to the firm. She took dictations from Niranjan and recorded and maintained minutes of meetings with clients. Apart from these secretarial duties, she met clients sent to her by her boss and prepared briefs of their cases and presented them to him before he would go headlong into the cases himself.

"This is a nice place for a quiet meal after a hectic day with the clients," Niranjan remarked sounding as casual as possible trying to put her at ease. Preeti was at a complete loss for words. She was overwhelmed by this sudden attention that she was getting from her boss. She fidgeted in her chair trying to adjust her *dupatta*. The recorded background music was soft and sweet. Pannalal Ghosh was playing the Yaman Raga on the flute. Niranjan had a taste for Indian classical music.

As a young man he had taken lessons, learning to play the violin. His teacher, Ustad Bashir Ahmed Khan was an adept musician. Dilruba was his chosen instrument. When he played the dilruba he could weave a spell that transported you to a world of pure magic. This great accomplishment of the Ustad heralded the doom for Niranjan's aspirations to acquire similar prowess. He was so disappointed with his own rudimentary efforts in creating music that he started neglecting his lessons. Instead, he would come to his teacher regularly but rather than picking up his violin he would plead with the Ustad to play a raga for the time of the day on his dilruba. The Ustad was so much impressed by Niranjan's love of music that he never failed to oblige. The music does not belong to the musician, Niranjan would tell himself, it belongs to the one who enjoys it.

They would sit on a large thick mattress that covered almost the entire floor area of the small room. A white sheet covered the mattress and they had huge cylindrical pillows for support or for reclining against. Niranjan would sit cross-legged surrounded by the sweet smell of incense. Enchanted, with eyes closed, some times with tears flowing down his cheeks depending on the mood of the raga, Niranjan would sit motionless as the maestro's bow massaged the strings and fingers of his left hand tickled them. The magical moment lasted at least an hour. At the end Niranjan would get up, bow his head at his master's feet and take leave. The maestro would get up, give his disciple a warm hug and let him depart in silence.

Today in a bizarre contrast of atmosphere, in this modern establishment, Pannalal Ghosh was trying to work up a similar spell. Presently the waiter appeared with two leather bound copies of the menu with the House's emblem in embroidered gold on the cover. He placed one in front of each one of the odd couple. There was one difference in the two menus. Only the one presented to Niranjan Dass had the bill of fare mentioning the prices.

Preeti did not say much; she was the quiet type and spoke only when spoken to, especially in the presence of her boss. He did most of the talking. If he said something that did not necessarily require an answer, he tried to figure out her reaction by looking at her changing facial expression or any other of her physical reflexes.

In his youthful days, Niranjan Dass was a debonair, tall, handsome man. He had a charming personality and likeable manners. His wiry athletic build gave him an Olympian aura. Once in those days when he was already a qualified lawyer he worked as an assistant campaign manager for a petty politician with high hopes. Mr Jeev Anand, the politician had provided Niranjan with a small room in his impressive mansion as an office. One bright and sunny winter morning when Niranjan was busy studying the voter lists, the politician's lovely daughter barged into his office like a whirlwind out of a clear blue sky and introduced herself.

"Good morning Mister…"

"Dass, Niranjan Dass." Neatly groomed and dressed in a blue blazer and silver grey worsted pants he looked very dapper.

"Good morning Mr Dass, I am Shweta, Mr Jeev Anand's daughter."

"Good morning Miss Anand. I am pleased to meet you."

Shweta was a tall girl with chiselled features and a dashing personality. She was wearing a collared red blouse with tight fitting blue jeans that seemed to add to her height. Her attire looked good on her. It gave her a fresh look of vigour and vitality. She appeared to be the kind of girl who was used to having her own way.

Shweta was the only child of the Anands. She had been pampered and totally spoiled since she was an infant. No wonder she grew up to be a reckless, headstrong girl. She made her choices independently and would never accept 'no' for an answer. Shweta took one good look at Niranjan and decided on the spot that he was the man for her. Her father, the politician lost the election by a wide margin but Niranjan Dass won the heart of Shweta.

"What else do you do Mr Dass, other than managing political campaigns?" Shweta asked facing him across the desk.

"I am a practicing lawyer, Miss Anand. I work independently."

"And what is your field of practice? Mr Dass, you don't have to answer any of my questions if you do not feel like. May be I am being too nosey." She was confidant he was going to answer all her questions.

"Not at all, Miss Anand. Please take a seat. To be honest, I haven't refused to represent any prospective client yet. I am trying to build a practice. Depending on the size of my clientele, when I am in a position to make a choice, I would like to be a corporate lawyer. But that may be a long way off. And how do you keep yourself busy Miss Anand?"

"Please call me Shweta. I have finished my B.A. at the JN University. I am planning to go to Cambridge for graduate studies in Literature."

If it was a fact that they were trying to impress each other with the glory of their assured future it was no less true that both were equally keen on being impressed by the other. They became instant friends and friendship developed into love. They started seeing each other regularly. Shweta's parents were very happy with this development.

As planned, Shweta went to England for her studies but she promised to come back to Niranjan as soon as she received her Master's degree. Niranjan received letters from her at regular intervals pledging her undying eternal love. The frequency of her mail decreased as time went by and then the letters stopped coming abruptly. She never came back and she never explained to him why.

Niranjan was devastated. He was still madly in love with Shweta but he never bothered to ask Mr Jeev Anand regarding her whereabouts or about her future plans. He came to the simple conclusion that she had met someone who swept her off her feet and that was the end of his love story.

Having lost the love of their life some people take to the bottle, instead Niranjan dug himself deeper and deeper into his work. Soon the routine of daily monotonous work overwhelmed him completely. Despite the success of his professional career he could not help but feel the hollowness that had claimed his life. He seemed to have given himself up to a barren existence which had no place for marriage and family. This meaningless humdrum of shifting gears between home and office would last for ever, it seemed. And he would accept it as the writ of his destiny.

And now he was sitting in front of Preeti in a seemingly romantic environment and he had no idea why. "Would you care for a spot of Chianti with your meal?" Niranjan asked Preeti.

"Pardon my ignorance Sir, but I don't understand."

"Would you like to have some wine with your meal?"

"I have never taken an alcoholic drink in my life and if you don't mind Sir, I would prefer not to indulge." She said apologetically.

"Don't tell me next that you are a vegetarian too."

"Sorry to disappoint you once more, Sir."

He ordered a carafe of the Italian red wine and topped up his own glass.

In deference to her vegetarian lifestyle Niranjan also decided to have a vegetarian meal.

"Let us order vegetarian. I think I shall have to eat twice my regular diet to make up for the protein deficiency. What would you like to have?" asked Niranjan.

"Anything you order Sir will be fine for me." Preeti assured him.

He ordered for both of them. As the food arrived, Niranjan passed to her one dish after another. She was taking very small helpings. Then having served himself he settled down to enjoying his meal. He watched her as she nibbled and munched on tiny morsels. Sitting in front of him she looked so delicate, so fragile. What a contrast to Shweta? He mused. She evoked fatherly feelings in him. Had there not been this gaping chasm of age difference, had he been fifteen years younger and she twenty years older, things might have been different. He would have no hesitation in kneeling in front of her and begging for her hand. In a fleeting moment the silly thought came and went.

Niranjan was sitting in his office poring over a file when there was a polite knock at the door. "Enter," he said. Manoj came in with Preeti on his heels.

"Is it urgent?" Niranjan enquired authoritatively.

"Sir, it can wait." Manoj said and turned to leave. Preeti also headed back for the door.

"And you Preeti?" asked Niranjan.

"Sir, as Manoj said, it can wait."

Niranjan assumed it would have something to do with the Ahuja case assigned to Manoj. He decided to get it over with.

"Come. Sit down. Manoj, you first. What is it?"

"Sir, we are getting married."

"You two?"

"Yes, Sir."

"Well, what do you know? And I never got a hint. When is the wedding?"

"This Sunday."

"Congratulations. You two have my blessings." Niranjan spoke avoiding an eye contact with Preeti.

"Sir, we would like you to come to the wedding. The ceremony will take place at Preeti's home. The address is on the card." Manoj handed over the wedding card."

"And Sir, Mom would like to ask you for a special favour." Preeti spoke shyly.

"Preeti, anything for your Mom. What can I do for her?" He offered enthusiastically.

“Sir, in the absence of my father it will make us all feel so much better if you could perform the *kanya daan*.” Preeti spoke pleadingly.

“I shall be honoured.” Niranjan was touched. Secretly he felt ashamed of what he had been thinking in the restaurant the other day about proposing to her. He was genuinely happy for them.

Forty four year old Sarla Puri was an attractive shapely widow. She had an oval face with soft-sweet features and a very fair complexion. Her thick pitch black hair rippled down the middle of her back in a loosely knit single braid. The fluffy un-knit end of the braid fanned out against her curvy hips. She had the largest black eyes that you have ever seen and they matched the colour of her hair. She was wearing a Punjabi style *Shalwar-Kameez* dress that highlighted the curves of her figure to perfection.

Sarla lived in a rented two room apartment with her daughter Preeti and her younger son Suresh who was studying for a degree in Commerce. Preeti was the sole earning member of the family and it was not easy to stretch her wages to cover the ever growing needs of the household. Sarla had a happy disposition and was normally cheerful despite being in dire straits financially. She had been hoping and praying that Suresh would complete his studies and get a job before Preeti got married. But Manoj had assured her that he and Preeti would look after the family and that she need not have any worries on that account.

On the day of the wedding Niranjan reached Preeti’s home early because he had no idea what giving the bride away involved. On seeing Sarla, he saw where Preeti got her good looks from, though the Mom was considerably taller than the petite Preeti.

Sarla was quite flustered and overwhelmed by the demands on her attention. She left Niranjan and Preeti so that she could attend to the last minute preparations.

"Sir, we are so grateful to you for agreeing to undertake this responsibility. We wouldn't know what to do without you." Preeti said when her mother was gone.

"'Sir' sounds so distant, so standoffish, Preeti. Can't you address me a bit warmly, a bit affectionately?"

"Like 'Uncle'?"

Half his wish had been fulfilled. He did not manage to grow any younger but Sarla was approximately twenty years older than Preeti. He was daydreaming again.

"Like 'Dad' or 'Papa'." He suggested to Preeti mischievously. He had no idea why he said that. It just seemed to have slipped out.

"For that I'll have to check with Mom first." Preeti blushed and gave him a warm demure smile. She was on cloud nine.

Before she could make a move to leave him, Niranjan spoke hastily, "No you won't. You will do no such thing, little girl. I do not trust you and I can't even trust Manoj for this one. I can't allow amateurs to handle this one for me. I shall do the checking myself. This is the one case I can't afford to lose."

*****

Shifting Sands

The income from my flower shop, Bloom 'n' Blossom on Bloor Street in Toronto was good and Mary, my shop assistant ran the business smoothly regardless of whether I was present or not. Because she was the one who dealt with our customers routinely, she was better known to the regulars than I was. She had a way with people and her winsome smile never failed to register. She was paid handsomely and she earned every cent of her pay packet.

Having emigrated from India and lacking education I had to work at odd jobs in Canada to make a subsistence living. Inability to communicate with the people around me was my biggest handicap. As a result I was forced to take up jobs that were temporary in nature, needed no particular skills and were therefore the lowest paid. I shifted from doing dishes at restaurants, toiling at suburban vegetable farms and working at road building sites. What I hated most was a watchman's job, sitting and staring at nothing in particular. Fortunately, I was well built and used to hard labor. I just could not stay idle. I could speak in broken English and spoke only when I had to therefore against my gregarious nature I became a loner which aggravated my feeling of homesickness.

By sheer determination and hard work over a period of approximately seven years I saved enough money to buy a small business. This is when Mrs Forster, the owner of Bloom 'n' Blossom decided it was time for her to retire. With a little help from the bank I was able to take charge of the flower shop. The rent of the store was very reasonable and the accounts figures showed that it was easily affordable. Mrs. Forster, a charming lady, agreed to work with me for a month or longer if necessary until I became familiar with the business routine. Mary, Mrs forster's shop assistant agreed to stay on making things even simpler for me. The income from the small flower shop was far beyond my wildest expectations. Now I could also find time to join some classes run by the Government to improve my spoken English.

The first time, I remember having seen Simmy, (I did not know her name then.) she was waiting at the bus stop not too far from Bloom 'n' Blossom. Mary had just hung the 'We are Open' sign inside the glass door. Simmy was standing in a queue. I had no particular reason to show any interest in her except that she was the only one of South Asian origin in the loosely formed line of commuters. Of medium height she had a remarkable figure with a beautiful oval face. Her free flowing shoulder length pitch black hair highlighted her very fair complexion. She was wearing a knee length maroon skirt with a cream coloured collared blouse open at the neck. Her unbuttoned coat was hanging loosely over her shoulders. She was carrying a good sized bag. Barring the fact of her probable Indian descent there was nothing to distinguish her from those around her except of course that she was singularly beautiful. I watched her board a downtown bound bus at 9.15 a.m.

When Mary remarked later that I was in an unusually chirpy mood I realized that I had been humming a popular Indian song repetitiously under my breath. I was feeling ebullient as if I had a date with the dream girl. It was foolish of me, of course.

Mary was still receiving the consignments of flowers from the delivery men the next morning when I arrived at the shop. It was unusually early for me and long before *the bus* time. Mary asked me casually if I had a good night's sleep. "Is something bothering you Kurt?" She added with concern. "Oh, I am fine, never felt better in life." I answered. I failed to mention that I reigned supreme in my aerial castle.

Sure enough, she appeared a little past nine a.m. Again I watched her from the shop. Only this time I stepped outside the shop but Simmy was oblivious of my existence. The bus departed at 9.15.

Then it dawned on me that if she was leaving in the morning everyday she must also be returning some time daily. I started keeping a silent vigil but without avail. The daily routine went on for some days. Mary had been watching everything without a comment at first then one day she said to me, "Good luck, she is unmarried and as yet not engaged."

"How do you know all that?" I asked her.

"She is wearing no ring to indicate she is married or engaged." She informed me. Mary had done some investigative work unnoticed by me.

Then one morning Mary sprang a surprise on me but more so on Simmy. She walked up to Simmy while she was waiting for her bus and presented to her an artistically put together beautiful small bouquet of flowers. I was stunned by what appeared to me Mary's daredevilry. I watched almost in terror. Simmy appeared to be taken aback by the sudden attention that she received not only from Mary but also from the other commuters who were exhibiting visible amusement. Simmy accepted the present hesitatingly. She seemed embarrassed and uttered something to Mary. I saw Mary turning and pointing at me. You could have knocked me down with a feather. Simmy looked in my general direction with a shy smile that lighted up her face as a couple of dimples appeared on her flushed cheeks. Mary marched back and shot at me, "This is how we conduct our business in Canada." I stood motionless as Simmy waved to me and boarded the bus. As if awakened from a deep slumber, I waved back, may be too late for Simmy to notice. I was still waving when the bus had disappeared. I entered the shop and looked at Mary for a long time. She was smiling impishly. I could easily have taken her into my arms and held her tight till doomsday. Instead, I announced a hefty raise in her salary. She pecked me on the cheek and thanked me. She was enjoying her role in the little drama.

The next morning Simmy walked up to me when I was standing in front of the shop waiting for her to appear. “Hi, my name is Simran Samra, friends call me Simmy.”

“Good morning, Simmy. May I call you Simmy?” I blurted out. At such close range she was stunningly beautiful. I found it difficult to look into her eyes. They seemed to hold a magic of their own.

“Sure you may.” She said simply.

“I am Kirtan Sangha. Everyone here calls me Kurt,” I said.

We started dating and got married within a month. Simmy was born and brought up in Canada. As such she had a completely western outlook on life.

*****

Uprooted from Jaisalmer in Rajasthan by Akbar, the great Mughal Emperor, approximately four centuries ago our valorous ancestor, a Bhatti Rajput warrior along with his wife and four sons, Basau, Raja, Abhu and Kalu for short, settled Raqba, our village. Each resident of our village is thus known by the name of one of the four sons of the Bhatti warrior. For example, in my village I would bear the suffix of Kaluka, meaning a direct descendant of Kalu; like a British person may be called d’Arcy or d’Urbervilles. In Raqba I am Kirty, short for Kirtan, Kaluka. Karnail Singh, a distant cousin and my childhood friend is called Kaila for short, Kaila Kaluka. Kaila and I grew up together; went to school together and dropped out after grade eight together.

Before my emigration to Canada Kaila and I spent most of our time together. He owned a medium sized mechanized farm. Being his only son he had inherited it from his father. He was a successful farmer using modern agricultural implements and techniques and was fairly well-to-do and respected in the village.

Kaila lived in the village like everyone else. He lived with his wife and his toddler son. He also had a good sized room with a veranda and a yard in his farm at a distance of about three hundred metres from his home in the village. This was his home 'away' from home where he could spend some time with his friends when he wanted to. This facility was built beside the well with a Persian wheel, reminiscent of days gone by. Now he also had a bored tube well at the same site. On a typical summer evening he would submerge a bottle of home distilled liquor tied in a piece of muslin at the end of a rope in the cool water of the well. Ice was not available in the village in those days and this was before the refrigerators appeared in the Indian rural homes. It was more fun drinking at the farm than at his home where his wife was always critical of what we considered to be innocent fun. My father was too strict to allow me to drink at home, let alone bring a drinking buddy with me.

Sukha, the carpenter was our age. He was still a bachelor and he was a real joker. Kaila, Sukha and I used to drink together and when we drank we laughed. We laughed at nothing in particular, but we laughed. Anything that one of us said was good enough for a laugh. And we laughed heartily, holding on to our sides. We did not have a care in the world. Sukha owned a prosperous workshop and I was assured of my inheritance of my father's farm. Lajo, my younger sister and I were the only children of our parents.

One day after a drinking binge at Kaila's farm, Sukha invited us to his home. We entered his workshop which opened onto the street. A door at the back of the workshop connected it to his home. Sukha lived alone with his father. Both his elder sisters were married and lived with their husbands. Sukha's mother had died long ago. His father was very old, frail and emaciated, almost bent double. He had been bedridden for some years. Sukha looked after his father like a dutiful son taking care of all the old man's needs. We paid our respectful compliments to the old man. He seemed to have already severed his links with the transitory world around him and was mindless of the goings on. We returned to the workshop to continue where we had left off at the farm.

With our backs resting against the wall we sat on the floor of the workshop where a good sized mat was spread. While he poured us our drinks Sukha said, "Friends, have your turbans dyed red. This is your official invitation to the wedding of my father. You know, I am looking for a youthful bride for my father. He will look so majestic riding a filly at the head of a marriage procession." And he went on and on. He was play-acting his father's imagined role as he waxed eloquent with his monologue. He was so funny with his childlike behaviour. We laughed spontaneously. We were rolling on the floor holding on to our sides. Sukha went on providing further details of the magnificent spectacle. Tears were flowing from our eyes when Kaila and I said goodbye and tottered out of the workshop heading toward our respective homes.

Overnight Sukha's father died. This was not what any of us was prepared for. We had no idea how to react to something like this. His father was not much of a companion as it were but other than his sisters who lived with their families in their respective villages, he was the only close relative Sukha had.

Kaila and I decided to pay Sukha a visit. But we were not sure we would be able to conduct ourselves in a proper manner. The three of us had never been sombre together. We had never been faced with something of this nature. We decided to take someone with us, someone mature enough to guide us through the testing ordeal. We found Tarlochan, Tochi for short, at home. He was a sober man with a melancholy looking face. No one in the village knew what his face would look like if it were ever required to display a smile because no one had ever witnessed that miracle. After some coaxing we prevailed over him to accompany us.

Kaila and I entered the workshop huddled behind Tochi. Most of the people were hovering around the dead body that was lying in the courtyard behind the workshop. We could see them through the open inner door of the workshop. In preparation for the cremation the body had been bathed and it lay wrapped in white calico.

On seeing us arrive, Sukha came into the workshop. We shook hands formally and sat down on the floor where a white sheet had been spread over the mat for the purpose. I was putting up a brave fight keeping in abeyance the vivid memories of last night. This was the first time in our lives together when the three of us were required to look sombre in one another's company. Tochi started the conversation by assuring Sukha that we were there to share his grief; that we stood by him for anything that he might need. I was avoiding eye contact with both of my friends. I did not know what I might read in their eyes. I was not prepared to take the risk. I did not dare to open my mouth and utter a few words of sympathy lest a word spoken might trigger the explosive that had been building inside me.

The workbench should have been removed and set aside. Most of the sympathisers and mourners were using a side entrance to the house but a few like us were using the workshop entrance and the workbench was lying in an awkward position and was in the way. Unwittingly, Tochi suggested that the workbench be removed from there. The Punjabi word for the workbench, *ghori*, is also the word for a mare or a filly.

On hearing the word, Sukha became tense. He stared at Kaila and he stared at me to see if we had caught onto the word; if we had taken the hint. Obviously Sukha was oblivious of the silly smile that unnoticed by him had got pasted onto his face. I had no idea what my face was saying but I seemed to be holding my ground. Quite innocently Tochi said insistingly, "Kaila, get rid of the *ghori*."

"Then what will the old man ride?" Kaila shot back. Unable to control himself Kaila covered his face with his hands as he bent double and laughed and laughed a muffled laughter. If a fellow mourner were to look it would appear like Kaila had broken down with grief and was sobbing his heart out. Like an arrow leaving the bow Sukha leapt forward and closed the interior door of the workshop. Unable to hold myself back I joined Kaila and laughed.

Having secured ‘Fortress Madhouse’ against the mourners, Sukha also joined us. Tochi was livid with anger. He hurried out of the workshop and into the street. “Go after him before he spells disaster for us in the village.” Sukha spoke with urgency. Kaila and I chased Tochi and caught up with him. “What was that about?” Tochi demanded an explanation. Kaila explained that the village pundit had warned us that no matter how miserable we were at the death of our friend’s father if we did not laugh at least once, the old man would go straight to hell. So we had to do it even if it tore our hearts apart. And the half witted Tochi fell for it.

Then I migrated to Canada. Seeing me wasting my time in India my father paid a ‘travel agent’ handsomely and got me an immigration visa for Canada.

*****

After our wedding, at my request, Simmy gave up her job as a receptionist at the law firm where she had been employed and took charge of the flower shop. The income from the flower shop coupled with the fact that we could depend on Mary to look after the business in our absence afforded us the luxury of an annual vacation wherever in this wide world we cared to spend it. But like a homing pigeon, year after year I kept coming back to India, where I was born and brought up. Cruises to the far off exotic lands were tempting. Vacation packages to popular destinations on the Riviera in South East France were hard to resist but I was too much attached to my joys and my sorrows that kept me bound to my motherland. The people with whom I had shared my pains and pleasures in my childhood and youth kept tugging at my heart strings and every year for a month of winter I ended up meeting the same friends and relatives. At the end of each vacation I would return to my home in Canada nurturing bitter sweet memories that lasted me the rest of the year to be renewed in yet another vacation. Having lived all her life in Canada, Simmy had little attachment for India.

Eight years after I first set foot in Canada, I along with my wife took my first vacation to the land of my ancestors. This was the only time that Simmy accompanied me on my trip to India and she was miserable all the while. Lacking sophistication, all my dear and near ones are simple country folk. They are all literate in Punjabi but most of them are uneducated by Western standards. It is only an odd one among them who can put some words of English together to make any sense. Simmy speaks or understands no Indian language at all. As a result she could not communicate with my elderly parents. Anyway, there was hardly anything common between them to talk about.

On arrival at my native village Raqba late in the afternoon, we found that Kaila and Sukha were waiting for us at my home. Each one of them held me in turn in a bear hug and lifted me off the ground. They were really happy to see me. After we finished tea Kaila said to me, "Kirty, your *bhabi* (meaning brother's wife) is waiting for you." To this my mother responded by inviting both my friends to dinner, which they accepted readily. Happy to see me after eight years, my father did not object to us to having a few drinks before dinner.

When my friends left, both my parents, my sister Lajo, Simmy and I sat together talking through the wee hours of the morning, though Simmy could hardly make any contribution because of the language barrier. Lajo was in grade XII and my father was busy looking for a suitable match for her. The sun was high up in the sky when we woke up. Despite my mother's strong protestation, I decided to have my breakfast at Kaila's. I did not offer to take Simmy with me because she had told me that she had no desire to associate with those 'louts'. Also I knew she would be totally out of sorts there.

I was glad to see my bosom buddy in high spirits. There was a huge tract of rich farmland worth hundreds of millions of rupees that Kaila was to inherit from his mother. But the offspring of his maternal uncle were cultivating it illegally. Kaila's lawyer had informed him that the law suit was going to cost a huge sum because the other party would like the case to drag on for ever so that they can get as many crops out of the precious land as possible while they were holding on to it. But he had absolutely no doubt in his mind that the case was as good as won. There was no possibility of their losing the case, the lawyer assured Kaila. The rest he said was up to the will of the Lord.

Kaila threw a lavish party that evening. It was given to honour my first visit after my emigration. But going by the expense involved, it seemed a sort of an advance celebration in anticipation of his imminent inclusion among the men of real wealth in the not too distant a future. "The next time you visit India, I shall have my Canada right here." Kaila assured me. "And don't forget to bring me a *mem* (a white lady) from Canada. As you can see your *bhabi* is advancing in years and wants retirement." And he laughed at his own suggestion.

It has become second nature now, the kind migratory birds have. Now I do not plan my vacations, I just book my seat, buy some presents for the dear ones and fly to India. Sometimes I wonder if someone had forgotten to snip off my umbilical cord, in a manner of speaking. Born and brought up in Canada, my wife believes I am wasting my time and money visiting 'relics of the dead past' as she puts it.

The next year I went alone. Simmy did not want to accompany me. I visited Kaila at his home. He was hardly recognizable. He had sunken cheeks and a famished look. There were dark patches under his eyes. Obviously he was undernourished. Four of his front teeth were missing. He seemed to have aged twenty years during the last eleven months. On seeing me he shouted to his wife, "Look Banto, God Himself has descended from heaven to visit us." While I held him in a tight embrace, my fingers ran over his ribs that were sticking out. I looked into his eyes and mused: This is the man who as a young lad could pin me down before you could count up to ten. I could not hold back my tears. As he offered me tea sweetened with dark brown lump sugar, he told me his sad story. He had sold the best part of his farm to finance the law suit which he finally lost. He had to sell all his farm machinery too. Apart from toiling at what was left of his farm, he had to accept work as a daily wage earner at other farms whenever he could find the opportunity. After he lost the case his wife gave birth to a baby girl. He named her Mangty (the beggar). With tears in his eyes he told me that his lawyer was one of the honoured guests at the victory celebration party thrown by his opponents in the law suit. He had been bought by them and unknown to Kaila, he had been working in their interest. Kaila felt that he was too naïve to survive in this age. "Kirty, what has happened to this world?" He asked me innocently.

At the end of my vacation, it was a tearful goodbye. I gave him all the money that I could spare at that time. I gave him a big hug and then he held my hand and won't let go. I promised to return the next year and departed. After reaching Canada I sent him money enough to last his family a year. When I tried to explain to Simmy why I was sending the money, she was hysterical. "You think you are some kind of a demigod or a saint. You want people to fall in obeisance and worship you. But you are making a fool of yourself." You cannot blame her. She was a product of the twenty first century western world, a selfish dog eat dog world.

My sister Lajo's wedding was scheduled to take place during my next visit. I arrived as planned. When I visited Kaila this time he was in bed. His wife told me that he did not recognize anybody. She spoke to him, "Look who is here. It is Kirty, your dearest friend." Kaila tricd to turn his face away but tears gave him away. Possibly he had detached himself from this cruel world while still living in it. I gave him an understanding smile and took his hand in mine. He squeezed my hand lightly and let go reluctantly. As if he had been waiting for me only to say goodbye, Kaila died during the night.

A Non-serious Misunderstanding

From Chandigarh to Parwanoo it is almost a level ride. But beyond Parwanoo the passengers jostled, as they were being thrown one against the other. The bus, traveling around fifty kilometers an hour, swung on the sharp curves of the winding Himalayan road. It gained from Parwanoo to Shimla over two thousand meters in elevation covering about ninety kilometers.

On any given day the coolies at the bus stand in Shimla outnumber the passengers. They crowd the arriving buses in such a manner that the passengers actually have to push and shove to break their siege and be on their way. If you make an eye contact with one of them he will hurl his official badge at you which implies that no other coolie will deal with you and he is the one you have to hire whatever his terms. The agents of the various hotels want your attention urgently while you are still in the bus trying to extricate your child from the pressing mob of disembarking passengers and before you can put your foot on solid ground.

Since the death of his father, last year, Kewal's mother had been badgering him relentlessly to agree to a marriage proposal that had been waiting for his assent. Kewal was only twenty four. He had an unmarried older sister. She was their mother's main cause of concern. The family was in no position to accede to the dowry demands of the eligible bachelors. Kewal's mother wanted him to marry first and bring in a sizeable dowry that could be made available for his sister's marriage. There was no other conceivable option. Kewal, an MBA, was not averse to the idea of marriage as such. Only he was not ready yet. And he was not too keen to jump into wedlock until he himself was settled in his chosen profession. He worried about his sister no less than his mother did. He had accepted a lowly job in a Shimla suburb while he was waiting for a suitable opening in a reputable business house.

Kewal was glad to get out of the bus and be on the road. He was lucky he was carrying no baggage and was traveling alone. After arriving in Shimla from Parwanoo by the last bus there was no option but to walk if he wanted to reach Mashobra that night. The option of spending the night in Shimla was actually no option because the price of an overnight stay in a hotel was far beyond his means. He did not have that kind of money on him and even if he did have it he could not afford to spend it. These hotels were far out of his league. He had no intention of staying in Shimla overnight. So he decided to hit the road. He took a few deep breaths before starting to walk up the Cart Road. Reaching the Mall Road he kept climbing up and was out of breath as he crossed the Scandal Point and reached The Ridge. He had gained considerable height above the bus stand by the time he passed the Snowdon (now IGM) Hospital.

The realization that he had not come for a stroll in the moonlight on the serpentine black tar road at this time could not deprive him from falling under the spell being woven by the fragrant night.

It was almost thirteen kilometers to his destination. But his helplessness was a sort of an enjoyable helplessness. The good thing was that he was not carrying any baggage except his light teardrop bag slung over his shoulders. The night was spellbinding; the twinkling stars in the inky sky, the rustling breeze caressing the whispering cedars. It was summer but late in the evening in this hill resort town it was pleasantly cool at seven thousand feet above sea level. He was young and exuberant and walked with urgency.

He crossed the settlements of Sanjauli and Dhali in a little over an hour. It was a heavily wooded route from hereon with hardly any habitation. The air was heavy with the scent of the forest. There was an intoxicating quality in the atmosphere. The tapping of his hard soled shoes on the road sounded out of place and alien to the environment. It did not seem to mingle with the scene. It sounded like a declaration of rebellion against the serene paradisiacal circumambience. He started walking off the pavement. It quelled the rebellion.

After Dhali there is a fork in the road. The road sign informed him that the road to the right led to the higher reaches of the mountains, toward the ski slopes of Kufri and further on to the greater heights of Narkanda. He took the comparatively leveler road on the left which the road sign indicated was the way to Mashobra. All the way from hereon to Mashobra there were steeply rising cliffs and slopes on his right and deep valleys on his left. He was surrounded by a thick coniferous forest on all sides. Most of the way from the fork onwards the music of the waterfall emerging from the bowels of the valley was sweetening his ears. The sound of the music was rising and falling with the contours of the road and with the whiffs of the light breeze. There was magic in the air. Moonlight was weaving a silvery charm and every aspect of nature was, in its own mute way, inviting him to a warm embrace.

His teardrop bag hanging loosely over his shoulders was caressing his back lightly as he strode towards '*Kahkashan*', Seth Hiralal's mansion. When he reached his destination his situation started bearing a question mark in his mind. Should he turn down the invitation to spend the night in the company of the heavenly bodies and in the pleasurable lap of nature in favor of a night in the uncertain hospitality of a host he had never known? But then a colder gust of wind made up his mind.

Light coming through the branches of the thick grove and '*Kahkshan*' written in large letters on the gate post assured him that this was his destination. But for these landmarks it would be hard to believe that humans lived there. The wrought iron gate in the boundary wall was locked but there was an unlocked side entrance beside the gate. He entered the premises. The atmosphere was the same inside as outside the gate; the same cedar trees, the same scented air. The difference was that his shoes instead of making a tapping sound on the road were making a crunching sound on the gravel covered driveway. Also now the air of abandonment that he had exhibited in his gait was absent. He was self-conscious and looking for clues to direct him from hereon.

A little distance ahead of him was a small clearing with a freshly mowed lawn. Between the flower beds was a fountain that was asleep. There was a statue of a maiden beside the fountain. Without paying much attention he proceeded further on the driveway. A cluster of trees came between him and the fountain. The fountain was again in his view as he passed by the trees. He stopped in his tracks. He could have sworn there was a statue beside the fountain a moment ago. His angle of vision had not changed that much with the few steps that he had taken. And now the statue had disappeared into thin air. What is more, suddenly the fountain had come to life and was sprinkling pearls against the tropical moon. If it had not been for the disappearance of the statue, there would not be anything mystifying about the fountain being switched on. He seemed to need a support even to keep standing. Had his imagination started playing tricks with him? Was this some kind of a haunted building? In a state of paralysis he saw it coming towards him.

"Who are you?" What he had imagined had been a statue demanded to know.

"I am…., well, Sethji has invited me," he blurted out.

"At this time?" She asked impolitely.

It was a tense situation. He felt like he had been caught stealing something.

"Well, in order to arrive at a decent hour I would have to spend the night on the way." He tried to explain.

Misty clouds emerging from the deep recesses of the valley were creeping up the mountain slope. But before a cloud could reach the summit a gust of wind would chase and scatter it. Within the valley below though, the clouds enjoyed comparative freedom.

"My Dad cannot see you at this time." She said firmly.

"It is OK. I can see him in the morning." He thought he was being very accommodating.

Sounds of laughter were audible despite the distance from the mansion from where they seemed to be coming.

"I am Sethji's new secretary." He tried to introduce himself to the young girl.

"So?" She seemed cold, aloof and unmoved by his statement.

"I reached Shimla by the last bus therefore I could not find any transport to Mashobra at this time. I made this journey on foot."

She folded her arms in front of her in a gesture of defiance. She was so close to him now. There was a distinct hint of a generous figure. The voluptuous curves of her torso, partially hidden in the mysterious shadows of semi darkness were well matched by those below and proportionately interspaced by a slender waist. She repeated, "Dad cannot see you before morning."

"Is there a hotel anywhere near here?" He asked, giving up.

"There are all kinds of hotels in Shimla." She spoke with a devil-may-care attitude.

Another burst of laughter from the building and then silence again.

"But Shimla is thirteen kilometers from here." He pleaded.

"That is so." She said matter-of-factly.

He felt he could not even keep standing. The energy seemed to have drained out of him. He rested his hand against a tree. In his agitated state involuntarily he started tearing at the bark of the tree. Startled, the girl's body became tense.

"Do I have to march back to Shimla at this time?" He wanted her to finally give the verdict.

"I am sorry but Dad won't see you before morning." She seemed to have mellowed down a little. She was almost apologetic.

"Can't there be any other arrangement?" He wanted to try his luck one last time.

"I am so sorry." She said sympathetically.

A misty cloud approached and enveloped them. It was almost windless now. Time seemed to have come to a standstill as they stood there.

"Will it be acceptable to you if I have to tread back to Shimla at this hour with my bag. I am already exhausted from the journey."

"It is so sad, but what can I do?" She was really sorry or she was an excellent actor.

"Can't I stay here?" He was almost begging now.

"There are already so many guests here. And what with the party going on. There is absolutely no room." She seemed to be at a loss for options.

The ensuing silence seemed endless. Maybe under the spell of the dream-world atmosphere, he moved closer and without knowing what had taken over him he placed his hand on her shoulder as he pleaded. She showed no resistance to his unexpected move.

"You must have a room of your own?" There is no harm in shooting in the dark as a last resort, he thought.

Silence again.

"Can't I get a little space to lay down my tired head?" Now he was pushing his luck.

As if sleep-walking the girl started moving in the direction of the mansion. He followed her quietly. At the back of the building the girl opened a door and signaled to the young man to enter. There were stairs leading up. Slowly and noiselessly he started climbing in the semidarkness. From some part of the building came another peal of laughter. Scared, he stood still. She was close by. He put his hand on her shoulder and followed her upstairs. At the landing she went through a hallway and opened a door. She led him in and after closing the door she turned the light on. For the first time he saw how beautiful she was. There was only one bed in the room. She turned the light off. Neither slept a wink that night.

It was still dark when he got out of bed and dressed up. He picked up his bag, came down the stairs, opened the door and went out. About a kilometer from *Kahkshan* he came to a spring where the water was cascading down the slope into a small pool before flowing into a steady stream. He took off his clothes and jumped into the small pond.

Having refreshed himself he dressed up and returned to the mansion. Seth Hiralal was making the morning round of his grounds.

"Good morning, Sir." The young man greeted Sethji.

"A very good morning to you, young man. What can I do for you?" The Seth said stiffly.

"Sir, I am reporting to assume my duties as your secretary." The young man said by way of an introduction.

"Ah! But you were supposed to come yesterday." The Seth said accusingly.

"As it happened, Sir, I arrived here very late last night and I did not think it would be proper to disturb you at that time." He tried to explain.

"And where did you spend the night?" The Seth was puzzled by what he was hearing.

"Sir, I went back to Shimla." He said brazenly.

"Did you walk back all the way to Shimla?" The Seth could not believe what he was hearing.

"It was all my fault, Sir. I should not have arrived so late." The young man wanted to shoulder all the responsibility for what happened.

"Young man, you should have at least informed somebody about your arrival. We knew that you would possibly arrive late at night. Accordingly, my daughter had herself prepared a suite for you. We were waiting for you." Sethji was really angry now.

"Sir, I thought may be you were entertaining some guests and I would unnecessarily be putting you through a lot of inconvenience. Anyway, Sir, I did not mind the exercise. It was very invigorating."

"What nonsense. Exercise, my foot! And what difference does an extra guest make in a building this size. Despite the guests there were at least ten rooms unoccupied last night. Anyway, your suite was reserved for you."

The girl appeared on the scene at this moment. Seth Hiralal Introduced the young man to her, "Rita, this is our foolish new secretary…" and he hesitated as he was raking his memory to dig out his new secretary's name.

"Kewal, Sir, Kewal Sharma." The new secretary said helpfully.

"Yes, yes, Sir Kewal Sharma." Said the Seth, laughing heartily.

"Glad to meet you, Sir Kewal Sharma." Rita joined her father in the fun. Kewal did not want to be left out, he started laughing too.

"Rita, show His Lordship to his suite so that he can get some rest and freshen up, poor devil." The Seth was still laughing.

"This way Sir, if you please." Rita led the way, this time to the front entrance of the mansion as he followed her obediently.

Madhav Dey, 0–2

It was the early fifties. It was the age of romance. It was the period of history when young men's eyes were still glued to the girls' faces. Faces, like that of the Helen of Troy, conquered hearts and bestowed sleepless nights on the dreamy youth of the male persuasion. The slightest hand to hand touch between the opposite sexes was very nearly enough to electrocute the love stricken in those days of love and romance. The innocent eyes of college going virgin boys had not yet learned to slide below the neckline; they fell on faces and stayed stuck there. (Teray chehray say nazar nahin hat-ti, nazaray hum suaah dekhen). The hour-glass figures were all there even in those blessed days but the southern component of their handle-with-care, explosive torso, the posterior, (derriere, as the British would have it) of the female body had not yet been thought of as being an interesting part of their anatomy. Even the facade had not yet been explored in any interesting detail. In a nutshell, a dreamy eyed girl like the late Bollywood actress Meena Kumari could have the figure of a column of the Indian Parliament and still enchant millions of her fans. The notorious Munni Malaika and the youthful Sheela Kaif were following in a long, seemingly never ending, queue waiting to be born towards the end of the twentieth century. I remember a film producer once telling me that he would never sign an actress for the lead role if she could not singly fill the screen with her presence.

We were innocent, not naïve, mind you, plain innocent. We thought we knew what there was to know about the human anatomy, male as well as the female. It was obvious, everybody had seen naked babies. Males had 'it' and females did not. Males had it at birth, this teeny-weeny nozzle for leaking. It did not grow on them. I mean it does not start sprouting later, after some days or months, it is there at birth as part of the delivery package. I do not mean to create the impression that it remains the same. Of course, it grows along with the rest of the body, sometimes, out of all proportions. Girls, on the other hand, were devoid of this itsy-bitsy protuberance at birth and failed to grow it later. We knew it. We were not blind to the stark realities around us. We knew boys were different from girls and that that was the sole difference. Boys were rightfully the proud possessors of something extra that girls would never have. The girls had nothing extra to show to match the boys' symbol of superiority, the leaky spout. So we thought.

Hens lay eggs and cackle; women lay babies and scream. So, what is the big deal, what is the hullabaloo about?

Hens and women lay eggs and babies respectively using the very same equipment; so we thought.

My friend Yog and I had passed our Entrance Exams and had joined college. We were both sixteen. One fateful day my friend's servant came to the Government College, Ludhiana. He had been assigned the task of bringing my friend home. It was Yog's engagement ceremony. Unmindful of what was going on around him, Yog was very happy. His bride to be was the daughter of a big industrialist, like his own father. I mean the industrialist like Yog"s own father and not the industrialist"s daughter like Yog own father. When the ceremony was over someone suggested to Yog to go, buy a book, Hidayatnama Khavind (Instructions to the Bridegroom) and read it. Yog wasted no time, got the book and sat throughout the night and read it. Overnight, he was a wise man. He had trespassed into a wonderland where no one our age was expected to set foot.

Early the next morning, bubbling with excitement, he came to take me to his home. As soon as I was within earshot, he declared, "Raju, girls have two." I did not understand what he was saying. Later at his home in the privacy of his personal quarters we sat, reading, looking at the detailed pictures and illustrations of both male and female anatomy, giggling all the while. For days after that we were exchanging meaningful glances. Overnight, we were wiser and more matured than the masses.

It was the age of innocence. The scourge of virginity was prevalent in epidemic proportions. It was here there and everywhere. Within your age group, you couldn't make a slight move without being hit by it.

It was also the age of Sahir Ludhianvi. He was no longer the local boy of the Government College of Ludhiana. Unmatched, he ruled the literary world of India. He had already published his Talkhiyan and Parchhaiyan. India swayed to the musical renditions of his lyrics. He was the poet of the century. Bollywood, as Bombay, now Mumbai, film industry is known, was madly in love with him.

If you were the college going youth of the early forties, you probably are not reading this; you are, in all likelihood, dead, unless you were forgotten by time and are looking (without sufficient sight) forward to hitting a century, which is no big deal. Like me, you are only being stubborn, not wanting to hand in your dinner pail and make room.

I was captain of the Ludhiana Table Tennis squad. The late Nimmi (Nirmal) Singh (RIP), by far the most handsome player in Punjab ever to wield a T.T. bat, was my Vice Captain and my doubles partner too. We were both in that class of players where we could make a splash here and register an upset there but could never win a singles title in a prestigious tournament. Just being a part of the show was fun enough. For me, being eliminated generally came as a relief rather than a disappointment. After that the tournament suddenly transformed from an arena of stress and struggle to a bouncy fete.

The six Dey brothers, in their heyday, packed more fire power in their repertoire of smooth-as-silk, forehand drives than the rest of Punjab put together; this, despite the fact that Cuckoo Dey, the undisputed Punjab State champion was not a member of this Dey clan. Sheetal Dey, the second youngest of the six brothers, even in the toughest matches, as his name suggested, retained a temperature considered below normal even for a healthy cucumber.

Madhav Dey, the reigning Punjab State junior, under 19, table tennis champion was a strapping, handsome young man, slightly on the plump side, though this feature seemed to have no ill effect on the subject's strappiness. (Don't reach for the dictionary, it isn't there.) In fact, it added to his charm for the opposite sex which happened to be the female gender in those days of yore.

Khullar, the long-range defensive player defied most of the rules relating to possibilities in that, when in action, he could be seen at various parts of the arena simultaneously. He could glide along the floor without making physical contact with it. I know what I am talking about. I have seen it with my own, presently macular-degenerated, eyes. He could easily have been a great ballet dancer if only he had an inclination for that fine profession. If you really wanted to enjoy watching him perform you would better cover your eyes to block the view above his waist and watch his legs weave their waltzing magic on the floor.

The manager of the tournament in Patiala was a rare diminutive homo-sapiens specimen. No one knew his real name. Everyone called him Machhar which was a misnomer because he was indisputably much bigger than a mosquito.

This was the first day of the tournament. My round one singles proved to be the non-event of the evening. No one had heard about my opponent. I eliminated him without breaking a sweat. Next, I was playing Madhav Dey, the junior champion. With his classic power strokes on both sides, he was the undeniable favourite. I was scheduled to meet him the next day. I had no more engagements for the rest of the day. On a balmy evening like this, you happen to be in Patiala, you have nothing to do and you are particularly not fond of twiddling your thumbs, so what do you do? Exactly. I just remembered that in my bag in my room lay that panacea, a pint of Solan No 1; I told Nimmi, the Vice Captain of our team that I was going for a couple of quick ones. I asked him if he would give me company. He declined my offer politely and wished me a merry evening.

Believe me, I am not using this as an excuse; it was a very long evening and by the time I was ready to say 'good bye' to the healer of all woes, the curvy flask, there was nothing in it to say, 'The same to you'.

Matches were being played in the auditorium. Nimmi saw me approaching, gave me a leery smile, got up, and disappeared. I went and took a seat in the stands. These were the preliminaries, there was nothing epoch making going on at the tables. Not knowing anything better to do, I just sat there.

It seemed tonight I had crossed the limit. Things were spinning around me. I don't know exactly how long I had been sitting there when I thought I heard my name on the sound system. A moment later the manager along with Nimmi stood in front of me. I realized they were both pleading with me to play Madhav that very evening, the match that was scheduled for the next day. Nimmi was more vocal in his pleading. 'Tight scheduling' the manager was trying to explain. He added that I did not have to play if I didn't want to. Nimmi jumped in and appealed to my sporting spirit. After my match I found out that the 'tight scheduling' was a hoax. It was all a Nimmi's brain child. He knew I was soused up. The fun, the spectacle of watching me play Madhav in a drunken state would not be forgotten in the near future. Where Nimmi is concerned a good laugh is worth a million stats. Rankings are mere figures while entertainment of this magnitude is rare. It was Nimmi who had planned all this. The manager was only playing second fiddle.

I got up, Nimmi helped me as he handed me my bat. My body swayed a bit as I tried to find my bearings. There seemed to be some disconnect between my upper body and my lower limbs. My torso had absolutely no desire to leave its moorings while my legs had a mind of their own. A straight line is the shortest distance between two points, mathematicians quote as a universal truth but judging by the distance covered by me from my starting point in the stands to the table may well be defined as a scenic route.

I placed my hands on the table to steady myself. 'Go Sidhu go' I heard Nimmi, above the din. I shot back something unprintable. By now everyone knew that I was being offered as the sacrificial goat, a drunken sacrificial goat. I could hear my name being shouted from every direction. Nimmi was the loudest. I knew I had been had and resigned myself to my fate as best as I could under the circs. I raised my hands above my head and waved to the screaming multitude. The response was a hearty burst.

I looked straight at Madhav. He seemed a bit blurry, somewhat out of focus. He is a lovable boy under normal circumstances. He was smiling shyly. I was still in the process of positioning myself in front of the table when Madhav served. I was at the table and before I could decide how to deal with the curvy orb, there was a flash of lightening. It seemed the ball had shot forward and it struck my bat forcefully.

Excuse me for digressing from the subject in hand a bit. I was going through this kind of shock experience for the second time in my life. The first time was when I was substituting in our college cricket team for a regular player who was AWL, (absent without leave, if you haven't been introduced to the term). I had never played cricket formally in my life. I was introduced into this match because the regular player who should have been playing wasn't among those present and I happened to be. I was the last batsman in and the team needed two runs to win. I was facing their star pacer, endearingly called Rapid Fire. I was scared out of my wits as I stood there lonely, abandoned by the world. I was scared and it certainly was not the fear of losing. I was concerned about my personal safety, exposing myself broadside as it were to this one-man firing squad. When I saw him running down the green he looked like a raging bull in a Spanish arena. Even the bat in my hands was not held firmly. I muttered a quick prayer. I did not see the ball coming but intense pain shot through my right hand and arm as the ball hit my bat. The bat shot off my loose grip. Luckily it missed the wicket. I could see the ball racing across the boundary line. My teammates and supporters swarmed the field. They lifted me above their heads and displayed me around like I was the trophy.

We have kept Madhav waiting. Let's switch back to him. Before Madhav's hand recovered from the elaborate follow through of his service the ball hit his left corner with the force that could have made a hole in the table. The ball disappeared in the crowd, you know, a case of hit and run. Just now I had executed a smooth down-the-line killer. Nobody had expected it from me, least of all I. I was a medium-long range defensive player. Madhav could not believe what he saw. We were expected to have long rallies with him hitting forehand-backhand strokes and I depending on my mean, variable back spins. But my legs were in no state to give a ballet performance. I had to stand my ground at the table and depend on half-volley shots as best I could. I had nothing to lose. Everybody expected Madhav to win. The next one he served on my left. I responded with a backhand smash across the table. Madhav looked at me. It was a baffled look. It seemed to be saying: Hey there, I am supposed to be beating the s..t out of Raju Sidhu. Who the hell are you? He could not believe what was happening. It was his nightmare. Having downed him 2-0, when I shook his hand at the end of the match it was limp like a wet rag.

Nimmi lifted me above his shoulders and for the second time in my life I was being displayed as a trop

When the Azaleas are Gone
(A novella)

When the azaleas are gone
Roses start blooming:
Seasons dictate so.
But do they?
One would wish so.

I

Strikingly beautiful, Geet Verma had emerged on the college scene like the glorious sun of an early spring morning. She was sixteen, peaches and cream complexion, rather self conscious and a sight for sore eyes. Well formed, slim at the waist, she was nimble on the foot. Let us put it another way: If Geet were to enter a beauty contest, she would in all probability be disqualified on the grounds of being overqualified. She was too angelic to compete with humans. It would be an odd male student or professor in the college who did not entertain amorous thoughts involving Geet. Going from high school to college was significant as it turned boys into men and girls into women overnight. She was only five foot four inches tall but she felt as if she had grown a whole lot during the last few months since she had said good bye to her High School.

This was a pastoral, laid back town where more than half its population depended on agriculture. It was rare for a freshman in this college to be able to speak a few words of English to make sense. Geet was fluent in English with an Indo-American accent, the result of Hollywood movies. The local cinema screened one matinee English movie every Sunday and Geet never missed it. Some locals who did not understand a word watched these shows anyway; it was fashionable.

Pampered at home, centre of attention in the college, Geet was living every moment of her life.

There wasn't a male heart in the college that did not throb for this demure arts student. She seemed to have invented charm. Everything about her made men want to hold and caress her. Young Joginder Gill, on his first assignment as a lecturer in History was no exception.

These were the good old pre-independence days when a Grade ten high school Matriculation certificate entitled you to admission to a professional school or college where you could qualify as a full-fledged doctor or an engineer with a degree. If you failed to qualify for an Indian Civil Service job a Masters' degree almost assured you a job as a lecturer in a college in a small town. Joginder Gill and Rajinder Walia had joined this college the same year. They were both twenty three years of age. While Jogi, as Joginder Gill was known to his friends, taught History, Rajinder or Raji was a lecturer in English literature. Most of the lecturers treated their first jobs in rural communities as internship, part of their training; stepping stones to jobs in Government colleges or positions in large towns that offer all the modern amenities and these two young lecturers were no exceptions. While they prepared their lectures, they dreamed of more prestigious and more lucrative positions in socially healthier environments.

While Raji Walia belonged to a middle class urban family Jogi had a prosperous agricultural background. Moonfaced Raji being the youngest and the only male of the three siblings was a bit spoiled and used to having his way in the family. Overall he had a carefree happy-go-lucky disposition. Overindulgence in food and lack of exercise were the basic ingredients of his lifestyle. He was short and plump, carrying a fair amount of fat on him. His job in this somnolent little rural town had brought him out of his family for the first time. He was born and brought up in Ludhiana, the native city of his ancestors and that is where he had completed his studies, taking his Master's degree in English Literature from the local

Government College. Raji was sophisticated and having passed his M.A. in the first division from this prestigious institution he had developed a kind of an attitude of superiority.

Erect and strong as a horse, Jogi, with chiselled features, was tall and narrow at the waist, built more on the lines of a champion sprinter. With his hard sculpted body he presented a total contrast to Raji. Jogi possessed as much athletic energy as Raji did not and that is saying a lot. Jogi was used to hard labour on his family farm which was no more than a couple of hours of bus ride from his college. Outside of the college this rural town where the two lecturers had started their professional careers did not provide a cultural or social environment conducive to a creative literary pursuit.

Geet came to know Joginder well but she was never conscious of anything but his casual interest in her as one of his favourite students. He was a dreamer who could keep his feelings to himself. Emotionally, he seemed to have the depth of an ocean that treasures its wealth rather than flaunting it.

There was nothing casual or dream-worldly about Professor Rajinder Walia's interest in Geet, though. His was a no-nonsense single track mind. He knew what he wanted and he thought he knew how he was going to set about getting it; the practical approach as you might call it, practical to the core.

Prof. Walia taught English literature. As such he already had an edge, a head start, if you will, as against, say, the economics professor or the professor of history, none of whom could lay layer upon layer of romance with dreamy eyes riveted to her face and still be completely professional about it. The advantage was inherent in his subject matter. Rajinder Walia was not supposed to teach Keats or Shelley while keeping a stiff upper lip. He had another advantage. He lived alone in a two room ground floor unit not too far from the college building.

Ironically Raji and Jogi became very good friends; goes to prove the authenticity of the age-old saying that opposites attract each other. Walia would boastfully share the secrets of his amorous conquests with Jogi: How he wooed her and how with the lure or rather the pretext of wanting to help her with her notes, he had invited her to his residence. When Jogi tried to bring up the question of morals, Rajinder brushed him off with:

"Jogi, take a look at her, it is a sin worth going to hell for."

Chubby faced Suman Kalia was the closest among Geet's inner circle of friends. She was plump and seemed to have retained most of her baby fat. She was Geet's constant companion and followed her everywhere like a poodle. She was also Geet's sole confidant. In the beginning Geet used to take Suman with her when she visited professor Walia. As Geet's relationship with Raji started warming up, she dropped Suman and started meeting him alone at his residence.

Soon the pretence of the notes was dropped and Raji and Geet became lovers. It is quite another matter that there was a huge discrepancy in the expectations of each of the lovers from the relationship. For the professor it was more of a cul-de-sac than an avenue that leads somewhere. You could go round and round a cul-de-sac as much as you pleased if you had no intention of going anywhere. He had no plans beyond what he was getting out of it. Geet, the incurable romantic, on the other hand, in her typical dreamy eyed manner kept holding tight onto the promise of a happy married life ever after. She was on cloud nine and Jogi did not have the heart to disenchant and bring her down to earth. Anyway, he was sure she would not listen to him even if he tried his best. Living in her own fools' paradise she was expecting to get everything that she wanted.

As is usually the case in such situations, there were two directly opposite opinions as to whether the professor had ever given her a reason to believe that the relationship would end up in a couple of

"I dos" and a happy ever after. He was sure of one thing, he was not prepared to be bogged down and be saddled with a wife 'until he had seen the world,' as he explained to himself.

Before she had given in to Rajinder's sexual advances, she had asked him if he loved her. And instead of making a commitment he had replied vaguely:

"You will never know love until you surrender to it."

Poor Geet, living in her castle in the seventh heaven, had accepted it as an assurance of his undying love.

Then one cursed morning, after about two years of a steamy love affair, she woke up to find that Walia had resigned from his job and had gone out of the town and out of her life without even the decency of a goodbye. He had, she found out, left the slow-paced old town to go to the Metropolis to accept the position of a lecturer in the Government college, his own alma mater.

Having finished crying her heart out, she sought Jogi and cried afresh just as a puppy having been kicked by an urchin would run up to his mother and seek solace in her lap. More than anything else she needed someone to stand between her and the big bad world out there. Suddenly, their affair and its tragic end had jolted the town out of its slumber. Everyone was talking about it. She placed her hands in Jogi's and sobbed silently. She had known all the time that he was Raji's confidant. Jogi's heart went out to her and he consoled her. Things have a way of turning out right in the end unexpectedly, he wanted her to believe. She looked into his eyes to find if there was any substance, any hidden meaning behind his words while he did not have the foggiest idea if he had implied anything more than he had actually spelled out.

In order not to give her any false impressions, he hastened to add: Life must go on, you know. I know it is not going to be easy for you but you must face life with a positive attitude. This certainly was not the end of the world. She could not afford the luxury of self pity. Her whole life lay ahead of her, he said, half patronizingly and half as a rebuke. Besides, Walia was not the only fish in the sea. He felt embarrassed when again she looked into his eyes, seeking to divine some meaning in the obscure generality of his words. Of course, Jogi pined for Geet. But having been hurt she was so vulnerable that any move on his part to come close to her at this time of her crisis, in his mind, would be like taking advantage of her.

Her hands lay limp in his as she sobbed silently for a long time. Like the calm after a storm, peace settled on her after she stopped sobbing.

Suman was the one who had asked Jogi to lend Geet the badly needed proverbial shoulder to cry on.

Not everybody was miserable because of Geet's tragedy, though. City police chief's daughter Sukhdeep was Suman and Geet's class fellow. Haughty by nature, she had sharp features and a fair complexion. She could not stand the sight of Geet. Geet was too beautiful to be liked or befriended. She brazenly gloated over Geet's disaster. She blamed Geet for "shamelessly peddling her hips around". Sukhdeep opined that justice had been done and that Geet had got her dues. She claimed that she had known all the time what was coming to Geet.

II

Geet was the daughter of a well known eye surgeon who practiced locally. Her two younger brothers studied in Bishop Cotton, a boarding school in Shimla, known as Simla in those days.

Geet never seemed to be able to live down her role in what was now the painful memory of her relationship with Rajinder. But she had learned to live with her sorrow and she completed her M.A. in English.

It seemed that for the five long years since that fateful day when Rajinder had disappeared each day was as empty as the one preceding it. Time dragged hollow as the morrow after having buried a dear one.

Having mourned her loss year after soulless year, Geet finally decided to say good bye to her past and agreed to marry an army officer ten years older. Handsome and full of youthful vigour, Major Jasbir Deol was a rich landlord. He had a lovable personality and was endowed with a sense of humour. At the time of their wedding he was on deputation working for the Government of India in Mussoorie, a popular resort in the Himalayas. On their first wedding anniversary Major Deol gifted the "Cedar Perch," to his wife. Cedar Perch was a beautiful cottage on the outskirts of the town. Soon after their wedding, Geet lost herself in the cosiness of Jasbir's embraces with the forgetfulness of a baby. He loved her ardently. She was quite happy.

This is when fate had brought Geet and Jogi together again. Still a bachelor, Jogi had taken up a job in a college in the same town.

Maya, a well mannered, unobtrusive local young lady attended to cooking and cleaning. She worked part time as she lived with her husband not too far from Cedar Perch. They had no children.

Babulal looked after the maintenance of the cottage and kept the garden in good shape. He had come from Bihar to the Deol farm at a young age and had served under Jasbir's father, Sardar Gurdev Singh Deol. Now after years of loyal service he was regarded as a member of the family. Inspite of Gurdev Deol's insistence, Babulal never agreed to get married. Since Jasbir received his commission in the Indian Army, Babulal moved with him wherever family accommodation was available. When the Cedar Perch was purchased, he moved in with Geet and Jasbir.

“I am glad to see you happy. Do you know a new angel is divinized with a pair of wings in heaven when an earthling puts on a smile?” Jogi said to Geet when they met.

Jogi was really happy to see her enjoying her life. Almost a decade after the curtain dropped on her accursed love affair she seemed to have finally buried her dead past to welcome her life with Jasbir.

Jasbir and Jogi hit it off together splendidly, the Major assuming the role of the big brother from the very start. The Major took a strong liking for Jogi and the trio started spending their evenings together at the Cedar Perch or at the Blue Room, “the Turned-Up-Nose-Club” as this elitist joint was alluded to by the locals. Jogi was always welcome at the Cedar Perch where he was a regular visitor. A phone call was sure to remind him of his absence if he failed to visit the Deols for two consecutive days. Routinely, there were three settings at the dining table even when Jogi was not present. As the tellers of tales would put it, for the trio this seemed like the ‘happy ever after’.

During the day when Jasbir and Jogi were at work, Geet spent most of her time in her study. Her study was a cosy haven lined with bookshelves against the two interior walls with a small music centre in the corner in between. The books among others contained library editions of British classics in fiction and modern American literature. The music collection contained the best from the great Indian classics which were the favourites of the Major while Geet had her own collection of popular film songs. There was a fireplace in one of the exterior walls and a bulging convex picture window in the other. There was a Van Gough print above the mantle shelf. An easel generally with an unfinished drawing stood ready in the corner between these two walls. The picture window presented a glorious view of the valley below and the majestic mountain ranges capped with timeless snow in the distance. There were a couple of easy chairs, a rocking chair and a large coffee table placed in no particular order.

Weather permitting, the favourite pastime of the trio in the evenings was to sit in the small garden of the cottage and talk casually about things that had no meaning at all, like the snobbery of the Chaddas or the obesity of the Rekhis; anything to elicit laughter. They would watch the beautiful sunset in silence before turning in. Snowfall in Mussoorie brings the child out of everybody in winter. The family would play with snow balls and make snow statues during the day and would sit by the fireplace at Cedar Perch stoking the embers in the evening. Usually on weekends Jogi would be invited to stay overnight, an offer that he never turned down unless he had some pressing homework to attend to. After dinner Jasbir would drive Jogi back up to a stone's throw from his residence unless Jogi preferred to walk back, which, weather permitting, was often.

Being young, exuberant and more or less carefree they planned excursions. Their first visit to the Kamptee Falls was especially memorable. Geet had insisted on carrying her own easel and painting stuff. With the easel and her haversack on her back she walked awkwardly with a stoop but she was in no mood to accept any help. It was a steady descent to the Falls and they progressed at a good pace.

As they came within sight of the waterfall, overawed by its beauty, they stopped in their tracks. The splendour of the majestic Kamptee Falls was simply ineffable. The water broke on the rocks as it cascaded down turning into a mist that blossomed into a rainbow creating a masterpiece under the bright sun. As soon as they reached the pool below the waterfall the men tore off their clothes and jumped into it in their brief underpants and started splashing while Geet planted herself on top of a rock on one side of the waterfall above them and got busy with her painting. When the men came out of the pool leeches were sticking to their bodies all over. It took them quite an effort to rid themselves of the parasites.

On the way back, Jogi had an idea; why take the long winding incline back to Mussoorie, why not head straight as the crow flies. The route, he thought would be shorter and it offered an element of adventure. They agreed to his proposal and started climbing up the steep mountain slope. Over the ridge of the hill and they started climbing down. At the bottom of this valley, to their utter frustration, they found that they were lower in altitude than the waterfall that they had left behind. And it was getting dark.

Here they came to a homestead with a lone occupant, a young Rajput man who happened to be sitting on a woven cot enjoying an early evening drink of liquor distilled by him on the premises. It seemed quite odd to his visitors that he was offering the liquor to his cow also who seemed to be habituated to the treat and was enjoying herself. The young man explained that drinking alone was not that enjoyable. Besides she was his sole soul-mate.

In his drunken state he was overwhelmed by the presence of such distinguished company. He offered what he liked to call, his guests, some of his moonshine which was politely declined. The young man was especially courteous to the lady who was totally out of his class. But the visitors were eager to move on because they wanted to be home before nightfall. They asked him how long it would take to reach Mussoorie if they stayed on course. It could take a couple of days, explained their host but mostly it depended on how fast they could move. He explained that it was not a straight ascent up to the town; there were many hills to climb up and down before the final ascent. The trio was sadly shaken by this revelation and they asked him what their best bet was under the circumstances. He advised them to retrace their steps and get onto the same path that they had taken down to the waterfall. They wasted no time in turning back.

Another untoward incident happened in the thick of the forest on their way to the regular route. They found themselves surrounded by a horde of shrieking black faced and long tailed langur monkeys swinging from the branches of the trees. They were threatening menacingly. Jasbir advised his companions that the best way to deal with the devils was to pay no attention to them. Soon they were out in the clearing and were glad to be on the right track. Once on the beaten track, they made steady progress. Still it was quite dark when finally they came within sight of their cottage.

The silvery moon was gliding over the sky, throwing a mantle of mellow sheen over the cottage perched atop the hillock. Once inside the cottage they poured their drinks and straightaway went to their bedrooms to freshen up and change into their pyjamas. There was no question of Jogi going to his own home that night. Jasbir came into the living room first. He had finished his drink and was laughing uncontrollably. Jogi and Geet also joined him. Jasbir pointed his finger at Jogi and said within peels of laughter:

"This man today wanted to feed us to the monkeys but the monkeys were perhaps too civilized to accept us as food."

For the rest of the evening Jogi was on the receiving end of a barrage of pointed jokes relating to his foolish suggestion of climbing straight up to Mussoorie.

Their trip to Cloudend was a totally different kind of an experience. It was Saturday and since they had planned to stay at Cloudend overnight they took their provisions with them. The descent to Cloudend was much steadier and they lost very little altitude. Cloudend was a privately owned bungalow being looked after by a caretaker while the owner lived abroad. The caretaker was quite obliging and for a small consideration he opened a section to the guests.

Cloudend was built above the edge of a cliff. The steep fall descended straight down to the expansive Doon Valley. Geet was especially ecstatic about the prospect of painting another great piece of art. After dinner they sat in lawn chairs in front of the bungalow, motionless in the stillness of the night, in perfect silence. It was a pitch dark moonless night and they gazed at the lights of the city of Dera Doon and the valley below as they rose to meet the twinkling stars at the indiscernible horizon. It was difficult to say where the manmade lights ended and the stars started. It was a mystic experience and they stayed there long hours. When they became conscious that the dew had started soaking their clothes, they moved in for their well deserved nightly sleep.

Then one day Jogi brought the news that would tear up this fabric of camaraderie that they had taken for granted. He told Geet and Jasbir that he was getting married to a Punjabi girl from the UK and would soon be moving there. They did not know how to react to this bolt from the blue but they congratulated him anyway.

III

Jogi had lived in the UK for twenty five years but the UK was never his home. Even though he had made a compromise on the bossy nature of his wife, he could never give any room to the interference of her parents in their day-to-day life. Having been the source of his immigration to the UK, his wife had always behaved as if she owned him and that she was the architect of his destiny. The bitter fact that her family had financed the convenience store that was the major source of their income did not help matters at all. It was a provision store in Wokingham with green groceries and a license to sell liquor. It also had a newspaper and magazine stand. It was a fair sized enterprise that paid well. His wife managed the store with the help of a salesgirl. They lived in the same building that had the store in it.

Jogi had a steady teaching job in a local county school. He had always felt that rather than being the breadwinner and the head of the family, his sole job was to service his wife and produce children. His usefulness in the family did not extend beyond this function. Having produced two sons, he felt that he had fulfilled that role successfully and was now an unwanted and even a dispensable appendage to the family. The realization dawned on him that with each day that passed he was becoming progressively unwelcome. He hated himself for having placed him in such a bind; and for what? What was it that his marriage had given him? His own two sons behaved like he was a stranger.

Jogi could have lived and raised a prosperous family anywhere in India on the revenue from his ancestral agricultural land in his native village. Loyalty to his estranged wife and uncaring children held him back while he lived in disgust of his surroundings. He had known it could not last forever. Things came to a head finally when after twenty five years of the charade of a marriage his wife handed him the papers seeking legal separation. She practically threw him out.

One beautiful morning he bade farewell to England and flew back to his native village where he found out with mixed feelings that there was no home that he could call his own. In his absence his two brothers had divided the ancestral residence between themselves. But his share of the agricultural land was there for him to claim. In a way he felt relieved because there was nothing to tie him down to his village. Culturally there was nothing in common between him and his brothers who lacked the benefits of good education. He knew he would be more comfortable if he could put some physical distance between himself and his siblings while maintaining the semblance of a relationship with them. In their own way his brothers were nice men.

He was quite sure he was out of the lives of his ex-wife and his estranged sons. But he was not so sure about leaving England for good. He had gotten quite accustomed to the charms of England, the ale-houses, the pubs with thatched roofs. The informal intimate atmosphere of most of the neighbourhood pubs that he used to frequent had infused in him a sense of belonging. And the people from the Indo-British community that he had come to know closely were some of the finest he had met in his life.

You could step out of the bustle of Southampton and drive through the thick blossoming rhododendron forests in the neighbourhood of vast stretches of heather that would not permit anything else to take root on its territory. Rhododendrons are native to the Himalayas but were imported to England from Spain and France a couple of centuries ago to adorn the royal gardens. Since then this species of purple, pink and white flowers has grown with tremendous success to claim the countryside turning it simply heavenly. If Jogi chose to live in England, his teacher's pension would be sufficient to provide for a decent living. But despite the companionship of his casual acquaintances, he knew he would be very lonely at home. He did not relish the thought.

IV

Misfortune, it seemed had taken a fancy for Geet. When the Government of India finally decided to complete the job of ridding the nation of the remnants of foreign occupation, Jasbir Deol, a colonel now, was called for active duty. Throwing the imperial power out of their pocket-holds of Goa, Daman and Diu was a minor and swift operation for the Indian army but at the end of it Jasbir Deol's body came home in a coffin.

Geet was in a state of total shock. She withdrew herself into her room, shying away from all human contact. She seemed to have wrapped herself in a cocoon. The five years that they had been married, Major Jasbir Deol had smothered Geet with his ardent love. Because of the taste of this love that she had become so accustomed to, her life as a widow was more painful than it had ever been before. Jasbir had left her to cherish fond memories in her heart and he had also left her with a most beautiful baby girl in her lap.

Babulal was in no better condition himself. He had swollen eyes even though no one had seen him crying. He sat down outside the door of Geet's room and refused to eat or drink. He insisted that he would accept food only after he sees Geet eating. Maya was miserable. She had lost an endearing master. The sudden realization dawned on her that she was to undertake the responsibility of running the household. She found out fast enough that she was not up to the job. She cried as she flitted around like a headless chicken. And yet she knew that she could not afford the luxury of breaking down.

When Maya informed Geet that Babulal had decided to starve himself to death, Geet gave up the comfort of her sorrowful retreat and came out to feed him. They sat in front of each other and shared food as they sobbed.

After Jasbir's death a thick fog-like sadness had settled on the cottage. For sometime Geet had persisting nightmares. One horrible dream in particular visited her repeatedly. She was hiding behind a bush in a forest. She had no clothes on. Wild looking armed men were looking for her. She could see most of them. She knew that they had already killed Jasbir. She was scared and breathless for having been running for her life. She was afraid they would hear her breathing. As she tries to shift her position slightly, one of them spots her. She wakes up screaming. She is breathless and perspiring all over.

She considered moving back to her parents' home. Her father had died a couple of years back. Her mother was still alive but in failing health. Also, the thought of giving up the Cedar Perch was too much to bear. She had too many fond memories attached to it. Everything nice that had ever happened to her in adult life had happened in Mussoorie.

She had asked Maya to sleep in her bedroom for some nights. Maya's cot was placed close to the baby's crib. Time, as they say, is a great healer. Looking after the baby was in itself a fulltime job.

Maya was very helpful. She was so attached to the baby it was not always easy to remove her from her clasp.

A sorrowful peace finally settled over Cedar Perch. Maya moved out of Geet's bedroom and Geet started spending some time with her painting. Babulal started bringing cut flowers from the garden and Maya arranged them in the vases kept in the living room and the master bedroom.

Geet never invited nor expected any company and yet she always kept two feather pillows in her king size bed. Once in a while she would take a Gin and Tonic before going to bed. On such occasions she would take off all her clothes hold the second pillow close to her bosom, shed a tear or two as homage to Jasbir before dozing off. But she never had an affair even though she was surrounded by those who tried to flirt with her. No man, she firmly believed, could fill the void left by Jasbir.

She decided to stay settled in the cottage in Mussoorie. It was serene and peaceful here. Because of the supreme sacrifice of her late husband, she had been offered a cosy job in the Department of Social Welfare, which she accepted gratefully.

Geet Verma, the heartthrob of the college in her youth had once been ditched by Professor Rajinder Walia. The experience had inflicted a wound on her psyche that would never heal. And now at twenty five she was a young widow. Nothing seemed to matter much anymore. A comfortable job, social acceptability, prosperity; she had it all but there was no antidote to the poison that had worked its way to the depth of her soul. She was content to lose herself in a sorrowful existence. She was particularly resentful of the independence that had been thrust upon her by the tragic circumstance of her husband's death. It burdened her mind with the need to make decisions, even minor ones like making a grocery list. She could do without these cares.

Happiness, she contemplated, she would not be able to recognize if ever she came face to face with it. But as time passed she decided to settle for peace. Peace seemed finally to have taken hold of all the hollow spaces in her heart. She did not care for happiness anymore, she just wanted to live and die in peace. If only she could go to sleep forever in her soft cosy bed, never having to get up and face the world. She wanted to be conscious of nothing except an interminable peace that would block out all memory of life as she had known. But then there was the cuddly baby, that fluffy bundle to care for. Juggling her job and the needs of the baby, Geet had her hands full. She settled down to bear her cross alone.

V

An outcast in England, an alien in India, Jogi was roaming on the main thoroughfare of Mussoorie, the beauty spot on the tranquil Himalayas. It was late in the evening and the street lights were shrouded in the misty clouds. It was drizzling lightly and the air was saturated with moisture. Jogi felt the cool moisture dripping from his hair onto his forehead. He paused in front of the imposing building of the Blue Room.

Membership of this exclusive club bestowed a special status, a kind of social acceptance that the patrons of this club enjoyed. But then you could not qualify for the membership if you did not have that status to begin with; the chicken and the egg story all over? The formal dress code here was never relaxed. The city's elite, gallant army officers, their winsome wives, administrators and their spouses and some ladies with not strikingly beautiful faces covered with layer upon layer of make up all gathered here for refreshments, their highballs and Patiala pegs. They came together to gossip, flirt and in general to ease their nerves rendered tense at the workplace or simply to shake up boredom.

Quite vague about what he was looking for, Jogi stood in the main thoroughfare of this hill resort indecisively. Mussoorie was experiencing a light drizzle. The locals like to address this beautiful hill spot as a 'she' and not an 'it'. Jogi loitered past the club, paced leisurely back and forth and then hesitatingly turned back and entered. There was a thin scattering of patrons in the thickly cushioned chairs. He could partially see the adjoining sunken anteroom. He stepped down into this cosy enclosure hoping against hope of coming across some familiar face. He glanced around casually. Not knowing anyone around, he climbed back into the front room.

The scene was familiar but after about a quarter of a century he did not expect to recognize anyone. He ambled up to the bar and taking a seat he asked the young bartender about his cronies of days gone by: Colonel and Mrs. Samant, Col. and Mrs. Rastogi, the Bassies. He could not muster enough courage to utter the one name that was uppermost in his mind. The names that Jogi mentioned made no sense to the bartender who was most likely born after Jogi last visited the club. He was quite apologetic for not being able to help, though.

A shapely woman in her early forties wearing a sky blue sari was standing near the window. The voluptuous curves of her torso, generously matched by those below were highlighted by her slender waist. She eyed him casually, then, as if on second thought she gave him an uninvited, almost a Mona Lisa timid smile producing twin sweet dimples. The smile seemed to say, 'Adopt me'. She reminded him of the puppy in the kennel, head tilted sideways, eyes oozing expectancy, 'Take me home, please.' The lady had a pleasant looking face with flowing hair black as a starless night. Another man in his position might have considered her a prize enough to 'go to hell and back for.' But Jogi just smiled in recognition without showing any intention of starting a fresh relationship, even a casual one. He would do well to first find his own bearings in his new surroundings.

There seemed little point in lingering but he did not have the heart to leave just like that. He had decided to come to Mussourie because his mind was occupied by images, with this club and Cedar Perch indelibly etched in his psyche as the backdrop to those images. Even so he had no intention of staying in this hill resort if he could not relate to it on a personal level; it could be the Queen of Hills or the Queen of Paradise so far as he was concerned.

Out of the Blue Room, he would be out of the city and in all likelihood, out of the country. In his present circumstances, there was not much purpose to his life in the UK either. But life in India would be unimaginable with nothing to relate to in this land. It would be less painful to drown his ever pervasive feelings of loneliness in the humdrum rumble of a neighbourhood joint in England. He was sure he could find some useful employment in the UK.

Unlike in India where everybody's business is everybody else's business the British are masters at leaving you alone. They seem to have developed it to an exact science. For an Englishman in the same room, you could just be another piece of furniture if not formally introduced. Except that they allow you some space around you which they shall not trespass and which a chair may not get. Of course you have heard that one in which the judge asks an Englishman why he had not tried to rescue the drowning woman, only to receive the response: But My Lord, we were never introduced.

Normally, in India the formality of an introduction is considered an avoidable superfluity. Here it is normal for a stranger to come up to your table in a restaurant and without even the formality of "May I join you?" sit in the chair opposite you when the dining room could be full of unoccupied tables. And before he shows any interest in wanting to know what you call yourself he would want to know what you do for a living and how much you make.

The other day when I got tired of climbing up and down The Mall in Shimla, I decided to rest my aching limbs for a while and took the only available seat on a roadside bench. Some young men were seated behind the benches on the ledge of the low wall that marked the boundary of a small flower bed well maintained by the municipality. One of the youths started tapping on the back of the moulded iron frame of the bench with the large ring on his finger while the rest of the gang started singing to his rhythmic beat oblivious of anyone else that existed on this planet.

As this ruckus was being played, comes along a gentleman and plants himself beside me but mostly on me because of the lack of available space. I looked at him trying to show my displeasure and he asks, "Are you a local or a tourist?", as if this was the main theme of the agenda. Without wanting to give him an excuse to make further queries, I volunteered that I had bought a cottage nearby and had paid seven million and three hundred thousand rupees for it. "Did you have it registered for the full amount or a smaller amount as is usual?" he insisted on knowing. Not wanting to risk getting arrested for having cheated the government of its rightful dues as stamp duty, I got up and made my escape while the going was good.

Joginder Gill, the object of our deliberations, was still in the Blue Room and could not summon the courage to leave. He was itching for an excuse to stay on. He could not just walk out and face the loneliness that was waiting to engulf him in the darkness outside.

"Can I get a cup of coffee?" He asked the barkeeper.

"Pardon my ignorance, sir, I have not seen you before. Are you a member?" The bartender was quite apologetic.

"I haven't been here in a long time," he informed the barkeeper. He knew the rules well.

"I am sorry, sir, but this club caters exclusively to the members and their honoured guests."

He seemed in no hurry to leave the premises. So many memories were buried in the dimly lit nooks and crannies of this old building. They hung as if midair all around him. His mind flitted from one to the other. He had all the time in the world and absolutely no idea how to beat it. Leisurely, he sauntered toward the exit door mincing his steps, wanting this walk to last forever. Had he seen something, rather someone? Almost at the door he looked back over his shoulder. He froze in his steps. She was looking at him intently. Her tresses, the length of an Indian widows winter night were cascading down her shoulders. Was he seeing a ghost? In a way he was, a ghost from the dead past. Could the few steps that he took back to meet her symbolize traversing a generation back in time?

"What are you doing in our world?" She enquired.

To him she looked like she was holding the sum total of the entire human misery in her heart. Her charming soft smile suffused with infinite sadness, seemed to accentuate the aura of her sorrow. He had come to know about her husband's death in action in Goa a long time ago. Dressed in shalwar kameez she looked girlish. Saris and sandals are not practical in the mountains. The dimples of her cheeks and her sensuous mouth seemed to have defied time and pain. At fifty, she was a shapely specimen of femininity. Her hair was a dark shade of grey, the same as the colour of her eyes, it looked glorious against her almost translucent skin. Jogi realized that she was beautiful as ever. May be his eyes could still see her in her virgin beauty as he had once known her in days gone by.

Did she mean "my world"? Not likely. It had never come to that.

They had not been mere friends. But then they were never much more than friends either. It was one of those nondescript kinds of relationships. Much in life can hang in balance, but for the want of a few words that remained unspoken; words, the indispensable curse of modern civilization. Words can be fascinating in print but in delicate relationships they can be used to camouflage or totally misrepresent feelings. But in the worst scenario, as in the case in point, words can spell disaster when not spelled out. A few words that she was dying to hear could have changed their relationship altogether. But that was all in the past. Now she could not imagine him in the role of a lover: Sex was not one of the ingredients that made up her life. She definitely did not think of him as she would think of a brother. May be an exceptionally dear friend on whose shoulder she could place her pulsating head and sob off her misery when life became unbearable; somebody with whom she could share a joke that is too explicit for mixed company.

"Geet, you are beautiful as ever. Time seems to have passed you by, leaving you untouched. You have looked after yourself well," he said hesitatingly.

"Drop it, Jogay, just drop it." (She was the only person in the world who addressed him thus. He was Jogi to all his other friends and relatives.) "You make a pathetic liar. It doesn't come naturally to you. So don't even try it."

Seemingly, Geet refused to accept the compliment even though she listened to his words like one listens to a sweet melody. Coming from him the words were the nectar that she had not tasted in ages. It was like the first drops of a bountiful rain on parched land.

"You can't just stand there and insult me and not even have the courtesy to offer me a cup of coffee." Jogi was ecstatic.

She ordered the coffee.

"And this is your world?" he asked.

"It is Queen of the Hills, what more can one ask for?"

“You know, Shimla lays claim to that title with equal zeal.” He reminded her.

“When were you in Shimla last?”

“That would have to be ages ago.”

“Nowadays it is not easy to walk on The Mall without stepping on dog-shit or human spittle even though Shimla administration still warns people of dire consequences if they dare spit on the roads. Do you know why the warning signs? Because spittle does not mix well with horse manure which covers The Ridge, the crown of your Queen. Except in the thick of the tourist season, scabies-ridden stray dogs with bleeding skins outnumber humans on The Mall on any given day. Women cannot take their groceries home without the risk of being attacked and robbed by monkeys that infest the town like lice infest a neglected human head. What queen are you talking about? Shimla, a queen? You must mean a fairy queen. Stupid, if you do not know what a paradox is, Shimla is a ‘he’ and not a ‘she’ like Mussoorie.”

His presence seemed to exhilarate her. She realized that she had not spoken so enthusiastically in a long time.

“Maybe our mighty Emperor Himalayas is not only a bigamist but is also bisexual.” Jogi sought to explain.

“How long will it be this time? You and India don’t seem to get along too well.” She was eager to know.

What was it that she was hoping to hear? Had she started building a dream castle again?

“Well, it seems like India will have to make some positive adjustments because this time I am going to stay put.”

Unwittingly, he had just now injected a huge dose of optimism into her frailty. She realized that she would be lonelier than she had ever been if he went out of her sight again. She needed his physical proximity even if he pretended to stay out of her life. Life had denied her practically everything that was worthwhile. Now even if life offered her happiness in half measures, she would grab it gratefully.

"What do you mean, 'stay put'?" She just barely managed to suppress a quiver on her lip as she framed her words.

"Exactly that, I am back for good."

He did not have the foggiest idea why or when he had taken this vital decision. All the same he had no problem convincing himself as he sat opposite her at the table that that was his well considered decision taken in his own best interest. His wife having received her divorce and his children having left the nest, as it were, he was now on his own, living a lonely life. Since he had left his family, his loneliness had been punctuated by an occasional spell of comparative happiness and that was all.

"You mean you are going to settle in India?"

"Now that is what I did not say. It is all up in the air as yet because I am not so sure about the settling part of it. Settled or unsettled will have to wait but I have no intention of going back to the UK."

"But as I understand your sons are settled there."

Having been grievously ignored and abused by his sons he had gotten into the habit of hungrily looking into youthful eyes anywhere seeking filial affection even if in short measure. It had gotten to the point where sometimes people considered his behaviour in bad taste if not outright depraved.

There was a long pause in which he seemed to have lost himself in thought and then he started speaking slowly as if forcing the words out one at a time. "They love it there. The UK is their home. They and their children have never known any other home."

And then as if wanting to get it over with, he added hastily, "Well, so far as I am concerned, they can have it and they can keep it all to themselves. I understand you have a daughter. Is she married or still living with you?" he asked.

"She is married to a doctor in the States. They have a daughter and a son." She said with visible contentment.

"Are you then living alone?" He asked.

"'Lonely' is my middle name." She remarked with a sad smile.

"At the same cottage?"

"The very same good old Cedar Perch. And where are you staying?" She wanted to know.

"The Gallery Club."

"You know you can't settle in a club. Excuse my using that word again. Where in India would you be living, since you are not going back to the UK? You have to have an address, you know."

"Drift: Free as a bird; I would like to drift, survey the beautiful landscape of this wonderful country, and keep drifting until something catches my fancy and holds me down." He decided to tease her. "You know, I never knew how beautiful this land was until I left it," he continued.

"When you are finished drifting and have an address, drop me a note, that is, if I am still around." She hit back.

"Why? Are you planning on moving somewhere?"

"Aren't we all? And stupid, you don't **plan** on moving heavenwards. Nature takes care of that. Thank God, there is one thing that you do not have to plan for. I think I would have to review that word 'heavenwards' because with my luck I will most likely end up in some flaming wilderness."

"Do you know that those of us who have paid off their karmic dues here shall be transported from their earthly abode straight to one of the choicest paradises because hereafter they deserve the very best," he said to comfort her.

"And there is this long stretch between deserving and having," was her response.

It used to hurt her when he behaved as if he had no recollection of the pain that this world had inflicted on her and now that he was reminding her of it, she felt that he was unnecessarily trying to bring her face to face with it and she felt the worse for it.

"I think you have been living alone too long," he said.

It seemed like ages after the death of her husband that a calm serenity had descended on her and had claimed her being. There was no uneasy mix of happiness or even of elation in this state of peacefulness. The impact of Jogi's arrival shattered that fabric of peace and serenity; like a piece of rock thrown onto the calm reflective surface of a lake in the wilderness.

VI

Jogi often looked back on his life in the UK. He would remember not with anger or even with resentment but with sadness how his family, his own flesh and blood, had abused and insulted him. In the evenings as they would get together, with whisky glasses in their hands, the agenda would normally be to rub their Dad's nose in dirt because, as they put it, he never amounted to anything. "Hundreds of thousands of Pakis like you have made it to England by marrying British citizens. What is so special about you?" they would taunt him.

His sons had thoroughly poisoned their own children's minds against their grandfather. Once Jogi tried to remind his older son of the sacrifices he had made for their sake. His son's wife immediately shut him up throwing at him a couple of words that she had likely picked up from some tv serial, considering that she never read anything informative. This, she declared was emotional blackmail.

His sons themselves had absolutely no talent except that of making money. They had expanded their business enterprises to the limit that they could handle but outside of their financial engagements their lives were devoid of any worthwhile interest. They had no books in their palatial homes, read nothing and had no taste in poetry or art in any of its fine forms. They participated in no games or sports and were never elected or nominated to hold a social or political position.

And yet his sons and their wives were ruthlessly cruel as they taunted him for being so insignificant. Jogi's English poetry and his short stories had been published by prestigious literary journals. He had been a member of the Executive Committee of the British Human Rights Commission as the sole representative of the South Asian-British community.

By virtue of having been the President of Indo-British National Association, he was once the Guest of Honour at an Indo-British Friendship Conference, where he and his wife sat at the podium flanked by the Mayor, the local MP, the President of the County IBNA and the local Councillor. As the guest speaker he spoke of the emotional turmoil that a sensitive immigrant has to go through. He had quoted that it was easy to take a person out of his country but it was not easy to take his country out of a person and that in his own case somebody had forgotten to snip off his umbilical cord. There was not a dry eye in the audience. Except his wife, his family were all absent from the conference attended by thousands.

Whenever there was an issue involving the Indo-British community, the TV camera crews would catch him, even at his residence to get his views.

Jogi remembered not without a feeling of pride the cases of two Indian sailors on two different Greek ships. A taxi driver of Indian origin had called him one night and had informed him that an Indian sailor had been badly beaten up by his crew mates and needed immediate help. Jogi went and met the sailor, Nichhattar Singh. Nichhattar was the only Indian member of the crew. It was X-mass night. Having beaten Nichhattar up the drunken sailors had gone to have a night on the town. While they were painting the city red, Nichhattar was left to guard the ship. Nichhattar sobbed as he told his story. He was abused by practically everybody on the ship who wanted to.

Nichhattar had been on the ship slaving for three years but was never paid a penny. Jogi contacted the Missions to Seamen at the harbour. The man in charge was shocked to hear the tale of woe. He was very sympathetic and suggested that Jogi should contact the Mayor. The Mayor immediately placed the ship under arrest and told the Captain when he became available that the ship would not leave the harbour until Nichhattar was paid his arrears in salary in full with interest. Failing this, criminal charges would be filed against the Captain and the crew.

After making some excuses, which were promptly dismissed by the Mayor, the Captain paid Nichhattar's dues in full. Jogi advised Nichhattar not to go back to the ship where he would run the risk of being thrown over board, once the ship was in international waters. With his wad of travellers checks secure in his bag Nichhattar, before boarding his flight back home, clung to Jogi with tears of gratefulness streaming down his cheeks.

The other case involved an Indian named Jagmel Singh who got badly burnt in an explosion on a Greek ship. Jagmel was told to undertake a welding job on the gate of the hold that contained coal. Jagmel who had never done any welding in his life told his boss that it was not his job but on the insistence of the boss he started welding. The built up gas in the chamber got ignited and exploded causing serious burns on most of Jagmel's body.

The ship had already left the harbour but was still in British territorial waters. The Captain refused to turn the ship back. There were five other Indian seamen on the ship. They revolted against the Captain who finally brought the ship back to the Harbour. Fortunately for Jagmel the nurse in attendance in the hospital was Indian. She called Jogi who got in touch with the insurance company. The company assumed full responsibility for the accident and agreed to pay all the expenses. When Jagmel came out of the hospital he was kept in a five star hotel for the recovery period. Having fully recovered Jagmel went home to India.

Despite the lack of support from his family, Jogi reminisced, he had done well. He was popular among friends and his services were appreciated in the community. He excelled in athletics and had coached the local youths. For some time he even hosted a TV show. His sons and their wives seemed to have gone into perpetual denial of his contribution in socio-political, athletic and literary fields. Whenever he was on the stage reciting his poetry or making a presentation, his children and their families were all absent. Once Jogi was called upon to recite a poem at a wedding party. His sons and their wives were all there. Before Jogi got up to speak, they left the party but returned for the next item.

Jogi had a couple of dogs, Pomeranians. He loved them to distraction. Emotionally, Pomeranians never grow old. They are known for their childish playfulness. When Jogi came home tired after a day's work, he would play with them in the lawn or drive out with them. Jogi's attachment to the dogs was reason enough for his wife and the boys to want to deal with them effectively. They had a simple solution for the "problem." His sons picked up the dogs and gave them to the first persons who would want them.

The boys were cruel to the point that they gave away the dogs to two different persons separating the couple who were from the same litter and had grown up together. Jogi had cried the whole night. The next day Jogi placed an ad in the local daily offering to buy back each one for a hundred pounds. Jogi never saw the male again. The man who had the female responded. As soon as the dog saw Jogi she struggled out of the hands of the man and ran to Jogi crying all the while. She was badly shaken and was trembling as she clung to him frantically licking his face at the same time.

The very next day the dog disappeared again. Jogi begged his younger son to tell him where the dog was. The boy lied to him saying that while he was driving with the dog she jumped out of his car and disappeared in the direction of the cemetery. Jogi had spent the night in the cemetery occasionally shouting the dog's name. He found himself totally beaten and all alone in the world.

His sons have always had dogs of their own.

One evening was especially painful. After Jogi had left for India for a short stay, Kamaljit, a very dear friend of Jogi called from Birmingham. Jogi's elder son answered the phone and informed Kamaljit that Jogi was in India. Thereupon Kamaljit asked him to send 'sister', meaning his mother to spend a few days with their family in Birmingham. When Jogi came back from India, his sons were itching to have a dig at him. If only they could make him miserable, it did not matter if they were insulting their mother in the process. Insinuating that Kamaljit wanted their mother for sexual favours, the older son said, "I wanted to say to him, 'Why don't you send your wife to me?' " The younger son interjected,

"No, not his wife, she is too old, you should have demanded his daughter." Jogi's older son's wife visits her friends, among them a taxi fleet owner and his wife regularly in Wolverhampton. But, to the best of Jogi's knowledge, his son had never demanded the taxi-man's wife or daughter in exchange.

There was a time when Jogi used to say to his friends with visible pride, "Having such wonderful daughters-in-law feels like having won lotteries." A close friend always retorted, "You feel that way because you are good yourself."

Even after he had said a final goodbye to the UK, insults followed Jogi. His younger son e-mailed, "Joginder Singh, I have decided to include you in 'my' family tree, implying that even though Joginder Singh was quite expendable as a sire, he, the offspring, in his extreme benevolence was prepared to bestow this undeserved honour on this man whom he addressed as Joginder Singh. He was implying that he was prepared to forego the option of having been born of Immaculate Conception, like Christ, the result of divine intervention.

There were hundreds of other incidences, one ghastlier than the other, some unmentionable, etched on Jogi's mind; each one a festering ulcer.

There is beauty and there is ugliness in every culture. Jogi's sons who had rejected everything good that the Indian culture had to offer, had grasped the worst and ignored the best of the Western culture. What appealed to them the most in the western culture was the brazen arrogance and lack of respect for old age.

For no particular reason at all, Jogi started reminiscing about his own childhood. He took a nostalgic journey to the lap of his grandmother, where under the fold of her shawl, he and his younger brother used to snuggle against her skinny body.

Jogi's grandmother knew only two stories. Every evening Jogi and his younger brother would insist on listening to the story of the cow's skeleton or the story of the singing tree. Grandma was only too eager to oblige.

Then one day when he was in High School, he was brought home to look at the body of his grandma. She was so beautiful even in death.

With sadness Jogi contemplated: His own grandchildren being brought up in contemporary British society may enjoy the benefits of all the modern amenities but they are not destined to experience the warmth of their grandmother's lap. Such is their lifestyle. Poor devils.

How far we have travelled, Jogi mused. He remembered with fondness how in the dead of the night, lying in bed, he would listen to the spellbinding doleful tune of the young man ringing through the darkness as he sang walking behind his oxen plying the Persian wheel. You could even picture him with his left hand placed on his ear and the right hand raised high in front of him for emphasis even though no one was looking. By the way, when was the last time anyone heard someone singing at the factory line? No doubt, we have travelled far, in the wrong direction, Jogi could not help thinking.

Outside of his family Jogi was loved and respected in the society in the UK and he had many fond memories. He was a member of the local Youth Association where, but for an odd exception or two, no one was seriously (to borrow a word from Bill Maher) religiulous. He remembered the *saropa* season at the local temple where the yellow rolls were doled out by the kilometre and measured by *dangan day guz*.

The problem with that social group was that you were required to laugh at the lewd jokes that you had heard from the same persons umpteen times. You knew the exact words by heart. People who had lived in the UK for over half a century never got a chance to replenish their repertoire of jokes with a Punjabi flavour. But the effort to laugh was a small price to pay for the fun.

Then there was the joker who had approached Jogi and in all seriousness had urged him to beat someone up for him. Jogi had wanted to know, "Why don't you do it yourself? You are yourself stronger than the man." With a straight face the clown had answered, "You know, I believe in non-violence."

On the whole though, out of the UK, he felt like a bird out of his cage.

VII

The Gallery Club, where he had set up his temporary residence in Mussoorie, was a no-frills classless type of an inn providing the barest of necessities in an informal environment. Having walked back to his temporary residence in this inn, he went into the bathroom to freshen up. He had already dined with Geet and there seemed to be nothing to do except going to bed. It was quite late at night but he was not sleepy at all. He was agitated and exited. He contemplated ordering a cup of tea but there was no one in sight. Noiselessly, he walked up to the front office which was deserted. He had not realized how late it was. It was past one O'clock. Unable to sit still and having no desire to lie in bed counting sheep, he decided to go for a nocturnal walk.

He got out of his small room and beyond the lobby he walked into the darkness past the Savoy Hotel. He left behind the unpaved pathway. Invigorated by the youthful scent of the night, he ventured onto the forest floor laid with a thick cushion of mulch that gave way under his feet. Above him a silvery moon was flitting through the branches of cedar and fir trees as he proceeded with an unsure step. Now and then a stray cloud would scud across the moon plunging everything into darkness momentarily.

He kept walking aimlessly through the tall virgin forest trying to calm his nerves. The countryside was wrapped in a mellow calm that can only be experienced in a Himalayan night. Everything around him had a subtle, almost ethereal quality. The world was steeped in a profound slumber. Apart from the dull sound of his footsteps, once in a while he would hear the hoot of an owl or the swish of a bird of prey in flight breaking the silence. There was something spiritual about the stillness of the scene. He seemed to have stepped into the Garden of Eden. He eased himself into a reclining position against a rock and lost all consciousness of time. Gradually he seemed to blend in with the stillness of the scene. Time hastened stealthily but he could not tear himself away from his surroundings that had perhaps remained unaffected by the global upheavals over the millennia.

He sensed that there was a profound primordial affinity between him and the serenity that surrounded him. He felt like a long lost baby who had finally been reunited with his mother's breast to savour the cosy security in the warmth of her bosom that rightfully belonged to him. One with the soft moist soil, the trees, the wet fern that was caressing him all over, he was a part of the sweeping sloping landscape. He wanted nothing to change ever when suddenly he became aware of the harsh reality of the night slipping away from the grasp of his senses and that he could not stay put.

Unlike in the plains, here the dawn, grudgingly surrendering to daylight, tries to hang on as long as possible. The transformation in the scene reflected itself in his mood as he was overcome by a feeling of abandonment. As the crisp early morning sent a chill up his spine he decided to turn in. There was a hint of the sun rising from behind the mountain.

VIII

Jogi went to pay Geet a visit at home. He could see the chimney of the Cedar Perch gurgling smoke into the atmosphere. Whiffs of light wispy clouds drifted against an otherwise blue sky. When he joined her she was busy pruning the low narrow hedge around the flower garden in front of her cottage. At fifty she still had a youthful effervescence unless his eyes were deceiving him. Maybe he saw her as he wanted to see her and not the way she was.

Babulal wearing a loincloth, burdened by the weight of his own emaciated skeletal frame was sitting on his feet and with his head almost between his knees, was removing weeds from between the tiles of a pathway.

After the death of Jasbir, Babulal had retreated into a shell. He had completely given up on sunlight ever shining on Cedar Perch again. He had shuttered himself behind a veil of dark despair of passive pessimism. He had never dared to dream of laughter ever ringing in the cottage again.

For domestic help Geet now had a young girl named Chhaili. Chhaili was an orphan from a remote village in the Himalayas in northern Himachal Pradesh. Her mother had died giving birth to her. She had been brought up by an aunt. Having lived her life in the Himalayas, she had no idea what the plains looked like. Geet had taken pains to educate Chhaili. As a result she had passed her grade X exam at the age of fifteen. Through a contact at her office Geet had even found a young school teacher who wanted to marry the girl as soon she was eligible and ready.

The sight of Jogi seemed to let a ray of hope peep into Babulal's feeble heart. He got up slowly and greeted Jogi with a beaming smile. Then he looked at Geet and again at Jogi trying to read something on their faces.

Chhaili had heard about Jogi from Babulal. Contrary to Babulal, at the sight of Jogi, Chhaili, who was normally very shy and uncomfortable with strangers, went completely berserk. A million *shehnais* started playing wedding tunes in her silly head and she seemed to have lost control of herself. "Beeji, look; look Beeji." Your Prince Charming has arrived, she wanted to add.

Squatting atop a hillock, the cottage with the gabled front of block stones was bathing in the afternoon sun. The roof sloped well beyond the outer walls. The thick foliage of the ivy crept around and in between the bay windows that were straining to peep through.

The lone cherry tree in the corner of the garden was looking down the slope of the hill. He remembered having seen it in an explosion of colour when it was in full pink bloom. Standing by its side one could see the lush green valley stretch below before climbing up the vast mountain slopes on the other sides. From this vantage point one had a panoramic view of the landscape. Homes with roofs painted red or green were scattered in the bowl below and on the slopes.

A couple of tiny hummingbirds birds had built their nest in the tree. Their frail looking chicks were always hungry. With their wide open beaks turned up they squeaked incessantly for food and greedily swallowed the morsels of insects brought by their parents. No matter how hard the birds tried they never seemed to be able to keep up with the young ones' hunger who kept crying for more.

A bird-feeder was hanging from a lower branch of the cherry tree. It was kept well stocked by Chhaili. A big rock near the edge of the property had a natural hollow on top. Chhaili made sure that it remained full of water at all times. The birds drank from this small pool and the tiny ones fluttered their wings and splashed as they sat on the edge of the mini reservoir and bathed in the sun.

"May I help you with the pruning?" he offered.

“I shall hold you in breach of my hospitality if you didn’t,” She quipped handing him the shears.

Geet left him and started feeding the squirrels without slackening her interest in the birds. She never tired of watching the birds enjoy their ritual splutter. It was her personal bird-haven, an open air aviary.

There was an inexplicable bond between Geet and the birds. It seemed like they could trust their chicks with her while they were out there gathering tiny morsels of food for the young ones. She could sense the loss of this faith when some guests were around. The birds fluttered noisily around the nest on such occasions exhibiting their discomfort at the aliens trespassing into their world. They did not mind Babulal or Chhaili, though. Do the birds react only to external human behavior or do they actually, in some mysterious manner, relate to human feelings?

There must be some karmic bond that brings souls together life after life to pay off their unsettled karmic debts, pleasant as well as unpleasant, and to create new ones to be settled in serial lives to follow until one blessed soul breaks the shackles and quits the cycle of transmigration to claim her abode in some eternal haven.

Jogi was fascinated as he watched Geet feed the little brown squirrels off her palms. How often, he reminisced, we let the little joys of life pass us by, joys free for the asking. How beautifully she blended with these heavenly surroundings, he marvelled. His mind completely overpowered by her presence, he went through the motions of pruning the hedge.

Some species of birds are senselessly noisy, chirping endlessly. Some, like the koel, spend most of their summer evenings wailing without getting any response. But there are those that seem to carry on a dialogue, generally one beseeching the other to come and join, not necessarily for mating, but for companionship.

A chick makes an effort to flutter its wings, fails miserably and falls out of the nest. Geet picked it up and tenderly placed it back with the other two. She seemed to be searching for traces of herself, her innocence, her helplessness in the activities of the chicks.

The tiniest of the birds, the shiny blue-green male and his brown female companion with their beaks almost as long as the rest of their bodies sucked the nectar from the depths of the horn-like morning glories, flying in fixed positions like baby hovercrafts. They were Geet's favourite birds. She was grateful for the companionship of the birds in her open aviary and kept them well fed. She was in perfect harmony with her environment, with the birds, the squirrels, the butterflies, Chhaili and Babulal. Compassion for the entire creation seemed to flow from her being as naturally as a fountain gushing from the mountainside bestowing life on the landscape that it touched. It would be torture for her to be otherwise.

Around the cottage was this interplay of misty clouds in the humid August afternoon. The valley below was drenched in sunshine where the roofs of the clusters of houses sparkled brilliantly while the tops of the mountain were blocked from view by the floating clouds. But nothing in the weather was fixed at this time of the year. Everything was so fluid. The beauty of the landscape owed much to the mercurial nature of the elements. Nothing lasted for too long; not the drizzle, not the misty upward flow of the clouds along the mountain slopes and definitely not the sunshine.

This was probably the best season in Mussoorie, if you did not mind the dampness. He enjoyed it immensely. The sun-splashed cottage seemed to be held atop the hillock as if it was planted there and yet it laid a sovereign claim to that spot in the sun with admirable success.

The wistful memories of the times, by far the best period of his life, spent in these environs had clung so tenaciously to his mind. He was overcome by the nostalgia of good old days.

He pointed out to her that there were not enough flowers to call it a flower garden.

"Well, so it happens to be. There aren't many flowers in my garden." She said pensively.

After a short interval she added, "The azaleas were in full bloom some days back but they have a pitiably short flowering period."

"Don't worry. When the azaleas are gone, roses will bloom. It is better that way. The cycle goes on."

"Silly, you haven't noticed; there are no roses in my garden. THERE NEVER WERE."

"Well, we'll have to do something about that. And I must confess it is hard to resist the thought of being surrounded by blossoming roses. You know, you need a good full time gardener. Hire me on trial basis."

"A senile old man with rickety creaking bones; a fine gardener you will make," she laughed as she made fun of him.

Instinctively, she hastened to ask, "And what about drifting, free as a bird?"

Enthused by her jovial mood, with a mischievous sparkle in his eyes and a melodramatic flourish, as if he were on stage, Jogi spoke:

"Like the Wise Old Man said: Woman is the cause of all sorrow in the world." He was intoxicated by her presence. Determined not to make any sense in what he was saying, he continued, "Now, have you ever seen a miserable man running to the court of law seeking divorce if there is no woman in his life, I mean, if he is not married? Why is it that only married men plead for divorce? They behave as if this is the last thing that they want to accomplish before they hand in their dinner pail. You want to know why? Isn't it obvious? I'll tell you why; because there is no woman making life a living hell for a single man. Geet, O Geet, I can't even divorce you because you never married me in the first place. What a pity."

"O stop babbling." She said with mock anger.

"I am afraid I have been stuck with this habit of being in circulation as a single too long to be able to remember how to conduct myself in the presence of a lady."

And as if he had suddenly discovered the panacea for all that ails humanity:

"Maybe the not so commonly practiced but the overexposed Amrita Pritam-Imroz living arrangement is the answer to all matrimonial problems," he declared without eliciting any response from her.

He was trying to make light of the matter that was gripping his soul.

She was bathed in a radiance that seemed to caress her like the sunshine. In his state of mind everything was enchanting as it revolved around her, the cottage, the garden, the balmy weather, the whole universe. Everything expressed itself as an extension of the focus of his attention. A feeling of delicious warmth permeated his being. Seemingly, interminable had been the nights that he had spent in bed awake, weaving hopeless fantasies. Blood now seemed to boil in his veins with quickened anticipation.

Chhaili served tea as they sat down at the cane table in lawn chairs. Perched on cloud nine, she was humming a popular Hindi film love tune as she went about arranging the tea set. She was simply intoxicated by Jogi and Geet being together. Her joy at seeing them together was so overpowering that she seemed to be bursting at the seams.

“What has gotten into you, girl?” Geet tried to pull her up.

Chhaili covered her face with her hands and danced back into the kitchen.

“She is really happy to see you,” Geet said to Jogi.

Babulal also saw it fit to leave them alone and disappeared into the cottage. Left alone Jogi took her hand in his.

“Hey, what are you up to?” Geet said mischievously.

“Don’t entertain any high hopes I am only trying to read your palm.” He said teasingly.

“Alright, tell me when I will land a young man, say tall, fair and twenty eight, to woo me.”

“Lady, ain’t you in luck, because you won’t get just one but two young men rolled into one, two-in-one as they call it, twenty eight plus twenty eight.” And she laughed uncontrollably flashing her pearly white teeth.

Geet felt a twinge in her heart. Happiness had always been there. All she had to do was to stretch her hand and grab it. It would have been hers for the asking. If only she had recognized it. Instead she chased a mirage. She had wasted her youth lamenting the loss of a love that never was. Raji was no more than an illusion.

In her presence Jogi did not at all feel in charge of his emotions. He was not sure of himself and he tried to hide his uneasiness under the cover of a carefree jovial verbosity. So much had changed over the years. She had gained in stature and strength of character. He himself had been rendered feeble and insecure by the circumstance of his own alienation by his family. At this stage of his life he needed her more than she ever needed his support. Her self-centred independence scared him.

They strolled in the narrow winding walkways of the small garden that held the cottage in a loose embrace. She walked slightly ahead of him as they talked casually. He studied her from behind. She was wearing a small cape over her shoulders. Romping on the mountain slopes gives a lady a strong back and legs but it robs her of her natural feminine grace. Geet proved to be an exception to that rule. She had the exact same figure, the same elastic graceful gait that he remembered so well.

They ambled up to the cherry tree as breeze tickled its top branches. He stood close behind her. Many were the times in the past when in the company of Geet and Jasbir Deol he had witnessed from this spot the western sky set afire by the setting sun. Held by the magic of the moment and a mutual bond, they would stand spellbound against the conflagration. All that seemed now to belong to another day and age and yet the fascination of that nature's masterpiece was etched indelibly on his mind.

He breathed long and deep. The moist air was lusciously heavy with the sweet smell of wild flowers mixed with the scent of the conifers. The intoxication pervaded the senses and penetrated to the depths of his soul. The setting sun was an enormous ball of fire. It slid behind the hill with the air of a princess stepping behind a curtain having said goodbye to her Prince Charming.

Even though only in flashes, he could not help think of himself as he was in the same environs the last time. Memories jostled one another for space. Nostalgia for the great times they had together welled up in his heart and he realized that he had never stopped loving her. There wasn't a mighty enough storm that the elements could muster to put out the flame that burnt within him. His chest ached with the desire to hold her.

When she sensed that he was close to making an amorous move, she remarked, “You are a joker, you know. Be serious.” And she knew he was dead serious.

“I have never been more serious in my life,” he claimed. Her soft dark hair shone in the bright sunlight like the back of a *koel*. Even at his age he feared he would burst out of his skin.

No one, she mused bitterly, not even God could compensate for the wretched days and the barren nights, year after interminable year that she had spent with longing to hear those goddamned words. Is this the man who would stand between her and her loneliness, between her and the cold world out there?

She turned around and looked into his melancholy gentle eyes in silence as she involuntarily touched his hand. Both were fully conscious that the current phase that they were going through was the late afternoon of their lives. But there was absolutely no reason for the evening not to be a pleasant one if the day has weathered a heavy storm. They owed it to themselves. For this moment in eternity, there seemed to evolve a complete harmony in their thoughts and feelings. For the first time they looked at each other nakedly exposing their souls. They were painfully conscious of the truth that a union between them at this stage of their lives would necessarily be shorter than it would have been if luck had favoured them earlier and yet it was no less true that the time left for them together was still going to be infinitely longer than no time at all: All the more reason that they should devote themselves to making each moment count in ensuring each other’s happiness. Their past misery gone through individually would be a guarantee that they would not miss out on a moment of the opportunity that providence had afforded them at last. He decided it was time to settle scores with their twin jumbled destinies and ensure their happiness as well earned mutual deserts. It was time to claim and to be claimed; to be held by that warm softness with its youthful face,

Overpowered by a suffocating emotion she realized that having been selfishly engrossed in the stakes of her own destiny, she had tried to block the stark reality from her mind that he adored her and had always done so, un-intrusively. Tears the size of monsoon raindrops welled up in her eyes. Jogi placed his hands lightly on the sides of Geet's face, barely touching her cheeks like he was holding an injured dove between them and looked sadly into her liquid grey eyes. He was feverish with longing and felt stifled by the missed kisses that seemed to hover around him.

"Twenty five years..." and she choked as she clung to him. Jogi wrapped his arms around her.

*****

www.ingramcontent.com/pod-product-compliance
Lightning Source LLC
LaVergne TN
LVHW010544160826
845677LV00013B/2990

9798374664140